The Eye of the Lens

THE EYE
OF THE LENS

Langdon Jones

THE MACMILLAN COMPANY
NEW YORK, NEW YORK

The Macmillan Company
866 Third Avenue, New York, N.Y. 10022
Collier-Macmillan Canada Ltd.,
Toronto, Ontario

The following stories first appeared in
New Worlds Quarterly:
    "The Great Clock" (March 1966)
    "The Eye of the Lens" (March 1968)
    "Symphony No. 6 in C Minor 'The Tragic'
        by Ludwig van Beethoven II" (October
        1968)
    "The Garden of Delights" (July 1969)
"The Time Machine" copyright © 1969 by
Damon Knight. "The Time Machine" origi-
nally appeared in *Orbit 5* which was published
by Berkeley Publishing Corporation.

Library of Congress Catalog Card
Number: 76-177438

First Printing

Printed in the United States of America

Contents

Introduction

THESE STORIES span the period from 1965 to 1969, and represent most of my output during this time. They are arranged in chronological order. The earliest of them is the most conventional in terms of both narrative and structure: although a couple of the later ones have a fairly ordinary narrative style, after "The Great Clock" the stories are structured in a more complex way.

I suppose that the main factor common to most of these pieces is a concern with the nature of time, a disease common to many writers of my generation. The present-day view of the nature of time is changing, anticipating rather than keeping pace with discoveries in the world of physics. This changing viewpoint is, perhaps, reflected in the difference between Wells' *The Time Machine* and my own. It might be said that the viewpoint of my story is a metaphysical one, but today it seems that physics and metaphysics are on converging paths. "The Great Clock" has a more conventional view of the problem, but perhaps its concerns are more with the fact of mortality than its cause. Similarly, "The Garden of Delights" has an old-fashioned, almost Edwardian, view of time travel, but it is in the peripheral implications of this theme that its real ideas reside. This particular piece is concerned more with possibility, with circumstance, with what would have been.

Time is seen with many eyes throughout this collection: as a tyrannical machine, as a fragment of a schizophrenic fantasy, as a purely psychological mechanism, having no objective existence, as a question of proximity rather than a matter of what is and what is not.

Two other themes accompany this concern with time and, to a certain extent, arise from it: the fantasies of schizophrenia, and various aspects of sexual relationships. Schizophrenics are possibly the only people left in the world who experience genuine fervor and a real terror of God. The fact that they sometimes see the reality behind the image, or the image behind the reality, seems to be leading some psychologists to regard these suffering people in such a way as to reverse the definitions of "sane" and "insane." But even if we disagree with this view, it must be conceded that these unwilling explorers are in the grip of what is less a disease than a religion. Apart from Olivier Messiaen, I can think of no artist working today, in any medium, who is producing works so filled with a genuinely religious fervor as may be found in the occupational therapy department of any mental hospital.

Love and death are the staple diet of the writer, each of them representing the acme of drama likely to be experienced by the average person in his lifetime. In love, one is closer to Huxley's "Antipodes of the mind," that raw world that hides behind the bland features of what we call "reality," than at any other time, and in the act of love it is possible to experience the suspension of time, the intimations of eternity that are daily fare to the asylum inmate.

But the purpose of both of these themes in my stories is neither didactic nor mystical—they are used rather as elements of a fiction than of an argument.

"The Great Clock" is, as I have already mentioned, the most conventional story of the book. It is also less successful than the other pieces, probably because it is more restricted in what it attempts. I have included it because it is a transitional story—the first to show some of the concerns that have since become a feature of my work, and I feel it says enough to warrant a place here. When it first appeared, it was notable in that it caused no controversy at all. The only point of contention is that no one likes its coda except me.

"The Eye of the Lens" caused me more difficulty than anything I had written before. The set of three stories was begun in 1965 and not finished until fifteen months later, but, owing to certain copyright difficulties, it was some further time before it saw print. This set was the first work of mine to abandon the conventional narrative and structure, and working on it was like trying to force a path through a jungle that was almost impenetrable. The stories were written in the same order as they appear, but each was created in a piecemeal way, especially the central one. The initial idea for the first story (originally planned to stand on its own) came when I was sitting on a District Line underground train on its way to Ealing Broadway—during the part of the journey that was, in fact, above ground, the train passed something I had never noticed before—a little brick building with a notice on its door which said: INTERLOCKING MACHINE ROOM. It seems unlikely that the mental picture this evoked corresponds in any way to the reality. The first story of the set is a reflection of the psychologist's view of the mind; it concerns itself with external events, but events common to us all. The second is partly concerned with external reality and partly with the internal, but this time the psychological landscapes are purely personal. The last story is completely external, dealing with myth and behavior.

In "The Coming of the Sun" I have used references

to, or quotes from, a number of sources, including René Char, Schumann, The Bible, Shakespeare, and Menotti. There are also purely musical associations. It is not necessary for the reader to look for these—if he happens to recognize them, all well and good; if he senses them unconsciously, even better. The first section to be attempted was "Black Wave, Take Me Away With You." The story was written in a totally nonsequential way, and did not reach its completed form until the third of five drafts. The section "Soleil de Sang, d'Oiseaux" was originally intended to consist of excerpts from Messiaen's own text to his choral work, the *Trois Petites Liturgies,* but the composer refused, on various reasonable grounds to allow this text to be used. The present substitute does not attempt to capture the unique atmosphere of simultaneous fervor and serenity which the original possesses. The figure of Schumann sitting at an asylum piano playing dissonant chords is based on the reality.

The final story, "The Eye of the Lens," was written in a state of righteous anger. It is permissible, I think, to use the device of the film—it is a "literary" film only; shown on a screen I do not think it would work. The section "The Eye" is intended to be the central part of the story, the trilogy, and the collection. A collector of symbols can label it as the eye of the unconscious, the eye that sees through the appearance of reality, the eye of the lens, the eye of God.

This trilogy of stories appeared first in the famous "banned" issue of the magazine *New Worlds.*

"The Time Machine" was relatively easy to write, and took only a few weeks. There are basically three threads of narrative running in sequence; the two subsidiary threads should not be searched for symbols. This story was originally planned for *New Worlds,* and reached proof stage before the printer felt he could not take the risk of publishing it, and the type was broken up.

The "Symphony" is in fact only an intermezzo. The points it makes are, I feel, self-evident. The final "poem" was born out of the accumulated amazement I felt after hearing many performances of the oratorio *The Dream of Gerontius*, Newman's appalling poem set to the most sublime music by Elgar.

"The Garden of Delights" caused the second and, I believe, final banning of *New Worlds* in Australia, by now hardly a surprise. The story was the germination of an idea I had carried about for some eight years. It took only five days from the initial planning to the finished type-script—the fastest piece of work I have ever done. It is purely fictional in design, and more notional than any of my previous works. The melodrama is intentional.

If the reader is unfamiliar with the nonlinear narrative, he would do well to remember that these pieces were not written to be searched for symbols—that is the job of the professional commentator; but on the other hand the reader's mind should not gallop away into the dim blue distance of free association. The stories should be read as conventional fiction is read, and if the reader feels he is missing something, he should blame the author rather than himself.

It is interesting to speculate on the direction in which fiction will be moving during the next few decades. Writing, in terms of a steady tradition of development, has lagged behind the other arts, possibly because its basic material is strictly utilitarian—if one had to write a melody for the milkman every morning, perhaps music would be in a similar position. But this does not alter the fact that it is essential for literature to develop in order to remain an effective means of artistic expression. Words have rich brocades of association, and carry behind them-selves the embroidered trains of their history; this is where the possibilities lie. I feel that a nonlinear or non-sequential narrative enables one to obtain the resonances and the extreme compression of poetry, to brighten the colors of language, and I believe this is how words should be used. There are too many writers at work today who would, it seems, reduce our language to a kind of binary system—on-off-on—and while this kind of work may have a surface facility, it is invariably long-winded, redundant, and ultimately devoid of meaning. I am aware that there has been a great deal of experiment in fiction, but one hopes that from those writers of what is being called "speculative fiction" will arise a coherent movement toward a new popular literature, a literature that will parallel the evolution of form and content that has already taken place in the other arts.

The Eye of the Lens

The Great Clock

1

THE LIGHT OF THE SKY could be seen dimly through the small slits in the ceiling of the Great Chamber.

The Great Clock worked.

The Pendulum swung slowly in its giant arc and with every tick, the whole Clock shuddered. The Great Wheel rose above the rest of the Clock mechanism in a great and static arc and the Fast Wheel whirled, humming, its sound rising above the noises made by the workings of the Clock. The other wheels turned at their various speeds, some smoothly, while some advanced one notch with every tick of the Clock. Pins engaged, wedges dropped, springs uncoiled. On the floor was thrown a shadow of wheels which formed an abstract pattern.

And the man sleeping naked on the pallet at the Posterior Wall stirred a little.

2

He was awakened by the whistle of the clock within the Clock.

It was fixed on one wall of the Great Chamber. It

was made of wood and the sound of its ticking was lost in
the constant sounds of the Great Clock. It was powered
by a weight on a long chain, the other end of the chain
having a metal loop through which projected the end of
a lever coming through the wall. At this moment the
lever, powered in some way by the Great Clock, was
lowering itself smoothly, pulling down the free end of
chain and winding up the clock. Below the clock, projecting upward from the floor was a four-foot metal flue pipe.
The whistle was coming from this, a deafening note that
was calling him to his duties. He covered his ears against
the raucous sound. Eventually the note began to drop
in volume and pitch, for a second broke down the octave
to its fundamental, and then became quiet except for
the hiss of escaping air. Behind the wooden wall could be
heard intensive creaking as the giant bellows exhausted
themselves.

The Clock ticked.

It was a thunderous sound, and it shook his body there
on the pallet. It was a sound composed of a mosaic of
sounds, some too high, others too low to be heard. But
the high sounds irritated the eardrums and the low ones
stirred the bowels. The sounds that could be heard were a
million. Metallic and wooden, high and low, muffled and
clear, they all combined in a shattering rumble that made
thought impossible. The tick was composed primarily of
four separate groups of sound that peaked at intervals
of about half a second. At the end of each tick, a creak
from somewhere high in the building ran up the scale
to silence.

When the echoes had died away he could hear the
other sounds of the Clock. The whole Chamber was alive
with noise. There were creakings all around; cogs met
with metallic clashes; wooden parts knocked hollowly.
From high in the Chamber on the opposite side to his
pallet the Fast Wheel hummed loudly.

He opened his eyes. Light was filtering in dimly through
the two tiny slits in the ceiling of the Great Chamber.
He could see the black outlines of the Great Wheel where
it vaulted overhead, partly obscured by a supporting
column. He groaned, then sat up on the pallet, looking
across toward the clock on the wall. The clock was made
entirely of wood, and only one hand pointed toward
the irregular marks scored around the edge of the dial.
The marks indicated the times at which he had to per-
form his duties; they extended three-quarters round the
face. When the hand reached any of the marks, the
bellows, now filling slowly behind the wall, would drop a
short distance and the metal flue pipe would give a short
call. The hand was about five degrees from the first mark,
and this gave him a short while to eat his breakfast. He
wondered dully if there was a little man inside the wall-
clock, just getting up, ready for his day's work maintaining
the mechanism.

The Clock ticked.

When the floor had stopped vibrating, he got up and
walked across the Great Chamber. Dust rose in acrid
clouds about him, making him sneeze. He urinated in the
corner, lifting his nose against the sharp smells that arose
from the intersection of the walls that he always used for
this purpose. Then he turned and walked back past the
pile of bones in the other corner, skulls like large pieces
of yellow putty, twigs of ribs, half buried by dust, and
made his way to the door on the far side of the Chamber,
moving among the bronzed supports of the Clock mechanism as he did so. He arrived at the low arched door and
turned the iron handle, pushing open the wooden slab
with effort.

The Clock ticked.

Now he was in the Small Chamber. The room was
about nine feet long by seven wide, and was lined by
wooden planks. The whole of the left-hand side of the

Small Chamber was covered by a mass of wheels, thousands upon thousands, interlocking in frightening complexity. He had never tried to work out their arrangement
and purpose; he just knew that they were an integral part
of the workings of the Great Clock. The wheels were
plain-rimmed—not cogged—and were of silver metal. They
varied in size from about four feet down to one inch, and
were all turning at varied rates. They whirred and clicked
softly as they worked. The sounds of the Clock were
muffled here in the Small Chamber, with the door closed,
and only the tick was still just as disturbing, as disruptive
to logical thought.

The Clock ticked.

He watched the chains from the wheels disappearing
through the myriad holes in the wooden walls at either
end of the Chamber. Some of the wheels were partly
obscured, with just a tiny segment of their arc appearing
through the space between the ceiling and the left-hand
wall. Once, he had wondered whether he saw all the
wheels or whether in fact there were more, many more,
stretching away upward and downward.

The rest of the room was taken up mainly by the only
compromise to his welfare, apart from the pallet in the
Great Chamber. There was a wooden table and a small
wooden chair. On the table were three objects, all of
metal, a plate, a spoon, and a heavy goblet. At the far end
of the Chamber by the cupboard set into the wall were
two silver faucets. Above the faucets were two wheels of
iron, to which worn wooden handles were attached.

The Clock ticked.

He walked across the Chamber and picked the plate off
the table. He placed it on the floor below the nearer of
the faucets. He stood up and began to turn the wheeled
handle. A white mash poured out of the wide mouth of
the faucet and slopped onto the plate. After he had turned
the handle about ten complete revolutions there was a

click, the handle spun free and no more mash came from
the mouth. He picked up the plate and carried it back to
the table, burying the spoon upright in the mash. Then
he repeated the performance with the goblet and the other
faucet, and filled the vessel with cold water.

The Clock ticked.

He settled down listlessly and began to spoon the mash
into his mouth. It was completely tasteless, but he accepted
it as he accepted everything else. The Clock ticked five
times before he had finished his meal. He left half the
mash and inverted the plate over the primitive drain in the
floor. Rotting food from previous meals still remained,
and at one time the stench would have appalled him.

A short, sharp blast from the pipe informed him that it
was time for his duties to start. There was a lot of work
in front of him. A vague memory came into his mind of
when he used to eat all the mash and still have a little
time to relax quietly before starting his work. Now he
toyed with his food and needed less.

The Clock ticked and dispersed the thought.

He walked with heavy steps over to the cupboard and
opened the door. Inside were his tools. To the left was a
rack of hammers for testing the wheels. They ranged in
size from a tiny hammer all of metal, the head of which
was about the size of the first joint of his little finger,
to a giant sledgehammer with a large iron head and a
thick wooden shaft, which was used for testing the Great
Wheel. The trolley was just as he had left it the previous
night. Everything was just as he had left it. The trolley was
made of black cracked wood with iron wheels. On it was
a giant drum with an opened top. A great faucet extended
down from the top of the cupboard above the drum, and
now the container was filled with yellow sweetly-smelling
grease. Every night it was the same.

The Clock ticked.

On a shelf on the right was a can, below yet another,

small, faucet, and the can was now filled by the dark
translucent beauty of thin oil. He lifted the hammers from
the rack and slowly placed them on the trolley beside the
drum. He lifted down the oil can and placed that on the
rack designed for the purpose.

He grasped the pulling rail and began to heave the
trolley backward out of the cupboard. His body strained
with the effort. Surely, at one time it had all been easier . . .

The Clock ticked.

The trolley was finally right out of the cupboard, and
he walked round it, so that he would be able to push it
from the back. Before he started pushing, he suddenly
realized that he had forgotten to move the table out of the
way. He sighed deeply and walked back to the table,
folding up the legs and resting it on its side against the
wall.

"Getting old . . ." he muttered, ". . . getting old. . . ."
Those were the first words he had spoken in a long time,
and his voice sounded thin and weak. He pushed the
trolley through the Small Chamber, past the whirring
wheels. His last duty of the day would be to oil those
wheels. He realized that he had forgotten to open the
door, opened it, and pushed the trolley into the Great
Chamber. He stopped the trolley at the point where he
always stopped it.

The Clock ticked.

He went up to the nearest of the wheels. It was a large
wheel, about five feet in diameter. Most of the wheel
could be seen clearly, unobscured by other mechanism,
and the black metal was pitted, as if by age. He selected
the correct hammer, a large one, weighing several pounds,
and swung it into contact with the edge of the wheel. The
wheel shivered, and rang like a gong. Satisfied, he placed
the hammer back on the trolley, and pushed it on a little
further. On he went, wheel after wheel. Some of the
wheels boomed hollowly, others tinkled like tiny bells.
Never had they done otherwise.

When he came to the first supporting column, he selected the second largest hammer. The column was of a diameter of about a foot, and it was made of a golden metal, either copper or brass. Later these columns would have to be cleaned.

The Clock ticked exactly at the moment he swung the hammer. But after the sounds had died away, the column still reverberated with a shrill brightness. Now he had come to the Fast Wheel. There was a wooden ladder set against its supports, and he picked up the oil can and began to mount the ladder.

The Fast Wheel was different from most of the others. It was difficult to observe, owing to its rate of travel, but the lack of fuzziness at the edges indicated that it possessed no cogs. It appeared to be a double wheel, having two rims, its spokes tapering inward to the single hub. It was driven by a taut chain which was an insubstantial blur that stretched to a hole in the Anterior Wall, opposite his pallet. The ladder vibrated with the wheel's motion, and air fanned his face strongly as he climbed upward. The wheel ran in oil, and a reservoir arched above it with two ducts that fell past its eighteen-inch radius to the hub. The hum of the wheel was almost intolerable at this closeness.

The Clock ticked and for a couple of seconds drowned the hum of the Fast Wheel.

He poured half the contents of the oil can into the reservoir, then quickly descended the ladder. Now there was just the Great Wheel and then four smaller cogs over the other side of the mechanism. He picked the largest hammer from the trolley and dragged it across the floor. The Great Wheel was only exposed at one point, and then only about a foot of its surface. This was about the nearest it was possible for him to get to the Anterior Wall. The Great Wheel was about a foot thick and was constructed of matt black metal; a foot from where it disappeared into the space between the floor and the Anterior Wall the

other mechanism of the Clock terminated. He dragged
the hammer into a convenient position and tensed the
muscles of his arms and stomach.

The Clock ticked.

He swung in an imaginary back stroke, the hammer
not moving, then, reaching as far back as he could and
starting to swing forward, transformed the stroke into
actuality by dragging the hammer along the floor toward
the wheel. The head lifted just before the hammer came
into contact with the black metal. It hit, and his stomach
was churned by the deep vibration of the Great Wheel.
Along with the almost subsonic fundamental, an upper
partial screamed briefly. The sounds almost made him
vomit, but he checked this and instead coughed the dust
from his throat. During the time when his duties had
always seemed to be much easier and quicker, and there
had been time to spare, he had watched the twenty-foot
Great Wheel very carefully for long periods, and had
never seen it move a fraction of an inch.

The Clock ticked as he walked away.

He went to his trolley and plunged his hands into the
drum, withdrawing two gobs of grease. He went up to the
Great Wheel again and slapped the grease into the
reservoir at its side. There would be more points to grease
later in the day.

Now there were just the other four cogs to test, and
then it would be time to check the Meter.

The flue pipe blew piercingly.

Shock raced through his body, and the grunt he made
was lost in the sounds of the Clock. *Had he been so slow?*
He never remembered having a job unfinished when the
time came to begin the next. He looked unbelievingly at
the clock on the wall; the hand stood unquestionably at
the second of the scored marks.

For a moment he was lost; his knees trembled and his
body shook. What should he do? Should he finish his job

or hurry to check the Meter? Normally he liked checking
the Meter; there was rarely any need to make an adjustment, the pointer always resting at the zero position. This
meant that he would have at least fifteen minutes to
himself. But now he was in an agony of uselessness, for
the first time being faced with a decision. A thought
began to bubble up through his shock, and forced itself
into consciousness for a fraction of a second.

Why?

The Clock ticked, dissolving the thought in a torrent of
sound.

He decided to check the Meter. He could always come
back and sound the remaining four wheels; it would mean
losing a little of the precious spare time, but that didn't
matter.

He wiped his greasy hands on his thighs and walked
across to the Posterior Wall and the little panel behind
which lay the Meter. He pulled aside the wooden panel
with effort, and then groaned in dismay. The pointer stood
at minus two.

He was plunged into panic; an adjustment would have
to be made. When would he have time to sound the
remaining four wheels? He would have to hurry. He pulled
aside the adjacent panel with trembling hands. He stepped
inside the lift and began to turn the large wheeled
handle. The Great Chamber was lost to view as the lift
began to travel down the shaft. Little light filtered down
from the Chamber, but he was able to see the joints in
the wood of the shaft. Going down, he was fighting the
counterweight and the work was much more difficult. He
wished that he was coming up, the adjustment having
been made.

After what seemed like hours, the dim light of the
Pendulum Well traveled up the open front of the lift and
he stopped.

The Clock ticked, very slightly muffled at this depth.

He clambered out of the lift and then finally stood upright in the Pendulum Well. The Well was vast. It stretched up and up, many times his own height, and the top was marked by a light rectangle where the mouth of the Well met the lighter Great Chamber at the very front of the Clock. Cogs jutted blackly above, and the tall cylinder of the Pendulum Rod inclined itself gracefully and slowly toward one side of the Well. Once he had wondered on the unusual nature of the Escapement Mechanism. The Escapement itself appeared to be almost independent of the Pendulum, its action only being triggered by the Pendulum's motion. The Pendulum swung freely for almost its whole arc, and the Escapement Lever only inclined at the extremes of its swing. At the top the Escapement Lever quivered, preparing for its giant pivoting movement, and its sound came to him like a clanking of great chains. The Pendulum had a wide arc, about forty-five degrees, and at the moment it was reaching the peak of its swing. The Pendulum was so vast that at this point of its swing it scarcely seemed to be moving. It was only when the Bob was whistling past his head at the bottom of its swing that he could really appreciate how fast it was moving.

At the top of the Clock the Escapement quivered again. The Pendulum had slowed now and seemed to be poised impossibly, hanging without movement, a vast distance from him. There was a rumble and, with a screech of metal, the Escapement Lever roused itself and began to pivot its great weight. With a shattering crash, it fell heavily into its new position.

And the Clock ticked.

Now the Pendulum was moving back again, increasing speed second by second.

The walls of the Pendulum Well were, like the Small Chamber, lined by planks of wood, although black. The sounds of the clock came to him here with a wooden

consistency as they were reflected and diffused by the
Well. On the near side of the Well, iron rungs were set into
the wall, which would enable him to reach the giant bulk
of the Weight. He glanced up, looking at the dark shadow
that loomed overhead. He stepped forward into the path
of the rapidly approaching Pendulum Bob, which would
pass about a foot above his head. At the far end of the
Well was another ladder which led up to a platform far
above, which would enable him to meet the Bob as it rose
up to the top of its swing, and from which he would step
on to the Bob to carry out the adjustment.

From its highest point, above the Escapement Mechanism, to a point about one sixth of the way down the
Well, the Pendulum Rod consistéd of a cylinder of shining
golden metal, probably brass, with a diameter of about
four feet. From there to the Bob, a distance of at least
fifty feet, it was made up of a frame of several smaller
tubes of various colored metals, probably some kind of
temperature compensation. The Bob itself was a ten-foot
lens of gray metal, tapering at the edges to knife-blade-
thinness. As the Pendulum rushed through the air, eddies
formed on alternate sides like the ripples running along a
flag, setting the Pendulum, as it rode the turbulence, into
vibration.

And the Pendulum sang.

A deep, clear ringing vibration filled the Well, like an
organ note, but with a chiming quality. He felt the vibration through the soles of his feet as he stood there on the
wooden floor. He kept his mouth slightly slack, for if his
teeth touched together they would buzz unpleasantly with
a higher version of the same note.

The Bob was now rushing down upon him, and with
a sudden gust of air, it was past him and away, climbing
rapidly toward the peak of its swing.

With a shock he realized that there was no time to
stand here watching. There were still four wheels left

unsounded. He turned and began to climb the nearer
ladder. There was a catwalk leading round the Well past
the Weight, and he always came this way to check on the
Weight as he passed. After a long time of climbing the iron
rungs he eventually arrived at the catwalk. The Weight
was a vast bulk to his rear; he was fortunate that he had
come down at this time, for often the Weight was further
toward the floor, or too high, which necessitated painful
maneuvering on the rungs.

He turned and looked at the Weight. It was a block of
black metal, about two feet deep and four feet high, and
it stretched the length of the Well. It was supported by
thin wire, which branched out from a single strand far up
the Well and culminated in hundreds of strands spread
out in an angular delta. At the top of the Weight was a
complex of cogs, the largest of which was about six inches
across, the smallest about half an inch, and some of them
were revolving quite rapidly. The fine wire passed up and
down in the complex of wheels, circling some of them.
These grooved wheels turned as the wire moved round
them, and the vast Weight was lowering itself, so slowly
that its motion could scarcely be seen.

The Clock ticked.

He glanced at the Pendulum, now at the fullest extent
of its swing at the far end of the Well. He would be able
to get to the platform in one-and-a-half strokes, by which
time the Bob would be in the correct position for him to
mount it. He began to move along the catwalk, his bare
feet pattering on the wooden planks. There was no safety
rail and he kept close to the wall, as he was now about
twenty feet from the floor. As the Pendulum overtook
him on its way back, the Bob dropped to far below his
level, and then began to climb past him.

The Clock ticked before he reached the corner of the
Well.

Past the corner he went, and he walked across the width

of the Well, a distance of only about thirty feet. The
platform projected out from the wall, and he stood out on
it, waiting for the Bob to arrive. There was a long, thin
chain hanging beside him, that stretched up into the
mechanism of the Escapement. He guessed that his weight
was computed by the strain on the platform, and pulling
the iron ring at the end of the chain caused some kind of
weight compensation to be applied to the Pendulum, so
that his weight on the Pendulum for one whole swing
had no effect on the accuracy of the Clock. The Bob was
now at the bottom of its return swing and was rising,
apparently slowly, toward him. Mounting the Pendulum
was a difficult feat, one that had caused him trouble in the
early days. The early days? He dismissed the distracting
thought: he must concentrate on mounting the Pendulum.
The difficulty was in the apparent motion of the Bob.
When one stood in the center of the Well at the bottom,
at the higher points of its swing the Pendulum scarcely
seemed to be moving, while at its center its true speed
could be appreciated. Here, at the high point of its swing,
the opposite illusion occurred, but was made more complex by the fact that the Pendulum *did* actually slow at
this point of its arc.

The apparent speed of the Bob was increasing rapidly
as it approached him. His muscles tensed as its bulk
loomed up toward him. He slipped his hand into the iron
ring, and pulled the chain downward. Then, as the Bob
was almost on him it suddenly appeared to slow. Now he
could see the corresponding platform that jutted out from
the Bob. He watched the platform and nothing else. The
edges of the two platforms came smoothly together. There
was a pause. He stepped swiftly across on to the other
surface. There was a brass rail on the inside of the platform with a strap looped from it. With fumbling fingers
he hurriedly buckled the strap about his waist and pulled
it tight, just as the Pendulum began to move downward.

And the Clock ticked, shaking the Pendulum.

He looked over his shoulder and watched the other platform and the catwalk moving rapidly upward and away from him. The acceleration became greater, and he felt his stomach lift within him as he traveled yet faster. The air rushed past his face, and he tried to draw his attention from the distressing physical sensations. The bulk of his body, tiny though it was in relation to the Bob, disturbed the flow of the air, breaking the current into smaller eddies. As the new vibration tried to impose itself on the old, the Pendulum groaned with tearing dissonance. Then, abruptly, the note broke up to its second partial, and the sound was now bright, ringing and intense. As the Bob began to level out, his stomach felt a little more normal, and he squatted down to make the adjustment. The platform on which he was squatting was slung at the lowest part of the Bob, and hung down below. At the very lowest point of the Bob was fitted the Adjustment Weight, for making the incredibly small adjustments to the frequency of the Pendulum's swing. A piece of thin metal rod was fixed from the Bob, hanging downward. This rod was scored across at regular intervals, about a quarter of an inch apart, and attached about halfway down was a small weight, of about an ounce, with a sprung clip that attached to one of the grooves in the rod. The Meter had read minus two; this meant that the weight had to be slid two spaces upward. Obviously the Clock was running slow by an infinitesimal amount, and this adjustment would correct its running. As he put out his hand the Pendulum began to rise on its upward swing, and his arm felt heavy and approached the weight much lower than it should have done.

He paused as the nausea gripped him again. After a few seconds the feeling began to diminish as the Pendulum reached its high point. He knew better than to attempt to adjust the weight at this moment.

The Clock ticked, vibrating the Pendulum, and almost
throwing him on to his back. He gripped the brass rail
and waited for the wrenching of his stomach as he fell in
the sweeping arc. The Pendulum began to move downward. The adjustment would have to be made this time; he
knew that he would be incapable of standing more than
one complete swing of the Pendulum. Air rushed past him
as he dropped with the Bob and he gritted his teeth
against the sickness that rose inside. At least the new high
note of the Pendulum did not buzz in his head as would
have done the fundamental. As the Pendulum leveled
out, he reached out and grasped the weight. He pushed
upward, and the weight moved up slowly with a double
click. He tested it with a light pull, and then sighed with
relief and began to stand, fighting the downward push
caused by the upward motion of the Bob.

At the top of the swing he stepped on to the platform
before the tick of the Clock commenced its vibration. His
legs were shaking as he began to climb down the iron
rungs.

As he walked across the floor of the Well his mind was
feverishly calculating. Would he still have time to sound
the wheels before his next task? He clambered down the
narrow tunnel into the lift. His next task was the Winding,
and he tried not to think of this. It was a task that took
about an hour of his time every day, and left him a weak,
trembling old man. Even so, he still sometimes wondered
how it was that such a comparatively small amount of
energy could sustain the vast mechanism all about him.
From his fuddled memory he vaguely recalled that on
similar occasions, the whistle had blown shortly after he
had arrived in the Great Chamber.

As the lift arrived at the top of its shaft, the Clock
ticked, the sound of it jangling afterwards in his ears,
contrasting with the sounds of the Pendulum Well. Here,
the noises were all about him again; the grinding of the

cogs, the humming of the Fast Wheel; the oil smells and the sharp tang of metal were in his nostrils again. His trolley was there, as he had left it. He began to walk across the floor, dust rising in clouds about him as he moved. He reached the trolley and grasped his hammer, ready for sounding the next wheel, and he used a small hammer that could comfortably be held in one hand. He swung the hammer and struck the wheel.

The whistle screamed, drowning all other sounds. He groaned out loud. The whistle stopped, and he stood there, hammer in hand, wanting to strike the wheel again. Why could not the whistle have blown one second later? At least he would have been able to hear this wheel. He almost swung at the wheel again, but he could not; it was time for the Winding. He felt tears springing to his eyes at the unfairness of it all. He was old, and tired. . . . He walked across to the Posterior Wall and slid open the panel that led to the Winding Room.

The Clock ticked.

This was only a small room and it was lined with planks like the others. It was completely featureless save for the Winding Handle which was set into the far wall and projected out into the room. He stepped inside and grasped the Handle. He put his weight on to it and it gradually moved downward, a ratchet clicking rapidly somewhere behind the wall. When the Handle was at its lowest extent, he slightly released the pressure and it rose up under his hands to its original position. He pressed down again. He would wind until the whistle blew again, a period he estimated to be about an hour, but a very long hour indeed. After the Winding he would be allowed a short time from his labor for lunch. Perhaps he could sound the remaining wheels in his lunch time?

The Clock ticked.

This would mean that he would miss his mash. He didn't mind about that too much; what really worried him was that he would miss his valuable rest period. The

handle rose under his hands to its highest position. He
was worried about the afternoon; how could he work if he
missed his rest? He was weak enough now. He pressed
down the handle. Sweat was beginning to run down his
forehead; he felt terrible. Surely, at one time he had not
felt so weak and tired. At one time?

At what time? For a second he was distracted from his
task.

He slipped.

His foot went from under him and he fell forward,
toward the handle. His hands slid from it and it swung up,
catching him under the chin and throwing him backward on to the floor.

Lights flashed under his eyelids and his head buzzed,
cutting out all other sound. When he came to he found
that he was standing in the Great Chamber, swaying
slightly.

Where was he?

For the first time his routine had been upset. The blow
had jogged his mind from its well-worn paths. He realized
that all the events of this day had conspired to open his
senses to this apocalypse.

He looked about himself in amazement.

All was as it had been; the Fast Wheel hummed to
itself and the cogs moved round at their various speeds.

But now the Clock mechanism looked alien and
frightening to him as he regarded it with eyes unclouded
by time.

How had he got here?

The stench of his own excrement arose from the corner
of the Great Chamber, mixed with the acrid tang of the
metal that surrounded him.

His head moved from side to side as he tried to see
everything at once.

The Clock ticked, unexpectedly, causing him to clap
his hands to his ears.

He had been so frightened; what had forced him to

carry out these awful duties that had wasted so much of
his life? He walked across to the far end of the Great
Chamber and looked at the bones in the corner. He could
see about four complete skeletons among the crumbling
fragments of many others. They were all supported on a
billowing pile of dust that came from innumerable others.
Were these the bones of the others, who, before him,
had tended the Clock? Did they, one day, suddenly know
that their time was up, and did they, obeying a dim and
contrived instinct, slowly, painfully drag themselves over
to the pile and quietly lie upon it? And then did the next
person come here and immediately settle into his ritual
of duties, ignoring the twitching bundle in the corner,
and later the odor of its corruption?

He walked back to his pallet and sat on it, burying his
face in his hands. When *he* came to the Clock, was there
a body in the corner? Did he sit in the Small Chamber
eating his mash whilst the air was full of the taint of
death?

What was his life before he came here?

Who was he?

He could not remember. Nor could he remember how
long he had been here. He felt round the back of his head;
his hair was hanging down almost to his shoulders. He
estimated from this that he had been inside the Clock
for a whole year of his life. He remembered something else.
His age. He was twenty-five years old.

Twenty-five?

Then why was he so weak and tired?

Something wrong made a shudder crawl its way down
his back. His hands had been registering something for
some time, and now he consciously accepted their message.
His hands told him that the skin hung loose and wrinkled
round his face. His hands told him that his features
were covered by wrinkled and flaccid parchment.

He sat up on the pallet in fear. He suddenly pulled

out a little clump of hair, bringing tears to his eyes. But
the tears did not obscure his vision completely, and he
could see that the hair was snowy white. He looked
up in agony.

"I'm old!"

The Clock ticked.

"I'm old . . ."

He looked down at his body. It was the body of an old,
old man.

He slowly stood and then staggered to one of the supporting columns. He embraced the column, resting his
cheek against the golden surface. His hand stroked the
smooth metal of the column's surface, almost as if he were
caressing a woman. He giggled.

"Look at me," he muttered to the Clock. "Look what
you've done to me!"

The Fast Wheel hummed; the cogs turned.

"You've taken my life! I was young when I came here a
year ago! Young! What have you done?"

His voice had become high and quavering and was
swallowed in the sounds of the Clock.

"Oh God!" he said, and slumped against the column.
He stayed there a long time, thinking. He was going to
have his revenge. The Clock would run down, with no one
to wind it. It would die, without him.

The Clock ticked, and he pushed his shoulders from
the column, standing erect. He began to walk round the
Great Chamber, putting out his hand here, stroking a
wheel there. He blew kisses to the Fast Wheel and ran his
flat hand gently over the surface of the Great Wheel.
Wheedling, coquettish, he minced extravagantly through
the Great Chamber, quietly talking to the Clock.

"Why?" he said. "Why? I've given you my life; what
have you given in return? You have taken eighty years
from me—what have you done with them? Are they stored
safely away in a cupboard? If I searched long enough,

could I find them, stacked on a shelf? Could I put out
my hands and slip them on, like clothes? Eh? Why did you
steal them?"

His muttering suddenly became ominous in tone.

"I'll fix you; I won't even give you the pleasure of running quietly down, as you would have done with me.
Oh no, my friend, you shall die violently; I'll show you no
quarter."

He moved across to the trolley. He painfully lifted off
the largest of the hammers and dragged it to the floor. A
wheel of moderate size, about four feet across, was quite
near to him. With all his strength he swung the hammer
in a low arc and relaxed only as it smashed into the wheel.
The giant hammer broke off one of the cogs completely,
and bent part of the wheel at an impossible angle. He
dropped the hammer, and, filled with emotion, crammed
his fists against his opened mouth.

The Clock ticked.

He found that he was weeping; why, he didn't understand.

The cog turned slowly, the damaged section moving
nearer to its inevitable interaction with another wheel. He
screwed up his eyes, and felt the warm tears running
freely down his face.

"I've killed you," he said. He stood, thin, bleached and
naked, paralysed and sobbing. Something would happen
soon.

The damaged section interacted.

The wrecked cog spun suddenly and rapidly before its
teeth engaged again. A shower of sparks flew out, burning
his flesh. He started, both at the pain and at the sheer
noise of that dreadful contact. At the threshold of his
hearing, far below the other sounds of the Clock, he could
hear the buckling of metal, the scraping of part on part.
The other wheel buckled and spun in its turn. A spring
burst from somewhere behind the wheel and scattered

metal splinters all over the Chamber. Strange smells were in the air; the death-smells of the Clock.

A trail of damage was running across the mechanism of the Clock like an earthquake fissure running across land. It could not be seen, and outwardly practically everything was normal, but his ears could hear the changes in what had been familiar sounds. The grinding and destruction spreading like a canker could be heard clearly enough.

The Clock ticked, and even the tick sounded slightly weaker.

Louder and louder came the sounds of invisible destruction. He stood, still weeping, shaking as if with fever. The changed sounds of the Clock plunged him into a new and unfamiliar world.

A different sound made him look up. Above him the Fast Wheel was running eccentrically. It was wavering from side to side in its supports, oil spurting from its reservoirs. As it spun, it whined, jarringly.

Abruptly it broke free of its supports and, still whining, it dropped to the floor. It screamed as it hit the floor and was covered by the roaring flame of its friction. And then it was gone, only the hint of a bright streak in the air indicating its trajectory. It smashed into the far wall scattering dust from the bones as the wooden wall dissolved into splintering wreckage.

An uluation came from the Small Chamber. Inside, the mass of wheels screamed as they were tortured by the new disorder spreading through their myriad ranks. The Clock shook in its ague, shivering itself to death. Suddenly through the open door of the Small Chamber came the wheels, thousands of them. The Great Chamber was full of smooth silver wheels, some broken and flying through the air, others rolling lazily.

The Clock ticked, gratingly, and then screamed again. The Escapement Mechanism jammed rigid, but the

Pendulum wanted to continue its swing. It did, bending
its great four-foot-diameter column in a grotesque shape.

Dust was everywhere, flying metal whistled about his
ears. As the sound became unbelievable the destruction
became complete.

His last sight was of light streaming brightly in as the
whole Clock collapsed in a mass of falling wood and metal
cogs.

3

And it was everybody else's last sight, too. They may,
for a brief period, have seen their world freezing itself in
grotesque lack of activity. They may have seen water,
solidifying in its fall to complete immobility; they may
have seen birds flying through air that was like treacle,
finally coming to rest above the ground; they may even
have seen their own faces beginning to register terror, but
never completing the expression. . . .

But after that, there was no time to see anything.

The Eye of the Lens

THE HALL OF MACHINES

*Many great thinkers have attempted to analyze the
nature of the hall. However, all their different approaches
have been characterized by a lack of agreement and often
blatant contradiction of fact. The appearance of the hall
is generally well-known, but as soon as we try to unearth
specific detail we realize that all is conjecture.*

*The hall is vast. We would expect the descriptions of its
contents to vary—one person could not be expected to
cover the whole area of its interior. However, there has
been a great deal of superstitious rumor concerning its
contents, and it is often difficult to separate the true from
the wholly fallacious.*

*There has been much conjecture concerning the size of
the hall, but no results have actually been confirmed by
any kind of measurement. It has been postulated by at
least one writer that the hall is in fact infinite in extent.
Others, no doubt influenced by exaggerated reports, have
maintained that the hall covers a variable area, its size
altering by a factor of at least fifty. Other evidence, how-*

*ever, suggests that both of these ideas bear, in all proba-
bility, little relationship to the facts.*

*During the last few years I have found it a rewarding
task to research all the material I could find that related in
any way to the hall. The task has been difficult, but
illuminating. I have now in my files a vast amount of
information in the form of books, articles, newspaper
cuttings, recorded tapes, and movie film as well as a large
number of transcribed interviews, on a subject which I
have found to become daily more fascinating. My research
has become, to a degree, obsessional. I now find that my
normal routine has been disturbed to quite a large extent
over the last three years. I have devoted a complete room
to this work, my ultimate intention being to shape the
material into a comprehensive book. All over the wall are
pinned the relevant newspaper cuttings, their arrangement
depending on whichever aspect of the hall I am currently
researching; set in the middle of the room is my movie
projector (frequently I watch the five hours of film I
have accumulated at one sitting), and beside it is the tape
recorder. On tape I have, apart from interviews and
commentaries, at least an hour of the recorded sounds of
some of the machines actually in operation. I have taken
these sounds down, as accurately as possible, into musical
notation. I have permutated the resultant patterns of
notes and have found interesting relationships between
the basic shapes, but, as yet, nothing more concrete.*

*I now spend a large proportion of my day in carrying
out this research. I sit for hours, cutting out newspaper
articles or developing film in the darkroom I have constructed. And so, with scissors, photographic chemicals,
music paper, paste, tape recorder, and projector, I have
built up a picture that is far from complete, but which is
remarkable in its specific detail.*

*I now present some of the more striking of the descrip-
tions I have unearthed. They are not delivered in a planned*

*order, but have been assembled to give, rather than a dry
academic account, a series of interesting impressions. I
believe that one of the most fascinating aspects of the
hall is in the diverse impressions it creates within the
minds of the observers.*

*When my book is complete (which will not be for
some years—it will run to at least five large volumes) I
shall have sufficient confidence in the correctness of my
results, and also the scope, to present them in detail. Until
then, these extracts are intended only to communicate
the atmosphere of the hall as it appeared to some people.*

The Water Machine

The troughs and gulleys of the Water Machine extend
over a very large area of this section of the hall, and
although it is enclosed by false "walls" of board, it still
gives a sprawling impression. All about are convex metal
surfaces; the floor is intersected by runnels and gulleys.
The Water Machine is constructed primarily of cast iron,
but certain of its parts are made of a lighter metal; probably an alloy, such as aluminum. The machine consists of
a complexity of large components which stretch probably
twenty feet in height, and the whole mass is supported
by a surprisingly small number of slim metal struts.

Water is being pumped in from a large pipe at the
very top of the machine. It is conducted by a series of
ingenious mechanical movements through a series of
gulleys and out of this part of the hall. I thought it likely
that the water was moving in a large enclosed cycle, and
dropped into a nearby channel a small piece of white
paper. As I suspected, within about three minutes, the
paper came floating past my feet again.

The noise of the water is almost deafening at times.

Constantly there is the hissing of the jet at the top of the machine and a rushing of the liquid as it bubbles its way through its course; also there is the loud creaking of the metal parts as they operate. Every few seconds there is an enormous crash as a metal part is activated, and the water momentarily redoubles its volume.

Water drips constantly from the supporting members, gathers on the floor, and runs down the slope toward the many drains: concrete channels sweep in graceful lines about my feet: cast-iron conduits curve in black roundness, globules of condensation running along their undersides.

Situated at the top of the machine is the vast silver belly of the top water container, spatulate and curved, like a vast silver spoon. The lead-in pipe, about six inches in diameter, is pointing into this tank, and a great jet of water, like a column of glass, is sluicing into its interior.

After a while, the container begins to groan, loudly. Suddenly the critical balance is attained. The groaning reaches a climax under the enormous weight of water, and the tank begins to shudder under a volume of liquid that it is incapable of supporting. Overspill slops to the floor and runs down to the square drains. Slowly, inch by inch, the tank begins to tip its vast bulk. Water spills over its thick pouring lip and falls in a glistening ribbon into a reservoir a couple of yards below. The tank begins to accelerate its rate of movement, and more water gushes down. Faster moves the container, and then, with a crash, it inverts itself. A solid mass of water falls into the reservoir, and the ground shudders with the impact. The container, meanwhile, is pulled back to a creaking vertical by a counterweight.

Water leaks from the reservoir, jetting out with great force from a circle of six holes at its convex base. These six separate streams are all conducted by diverse methods to the ground. One of the streams gushes into a smaller version of the water-barrel. Another enters one of the

hinged containers set between the double rim of a large
wheel, its weight causing the wheel to rotate slowly; after
a quarter-revolution the container will snag on a projection
and tip up, letting the water escape into one of the channels. Another stream strikes a sprung flange which bounces
constantly in and out of the flow, the other end of the
flange operating a mechanism like the escapement of a
clock.

All the streams eventually reach the dark channels of
wet concrete set in the floor, and are then conducted away
from sight through holes set in the surrounding "walls."

Behind the wall can be heard the sound of great pumps.

Up above, I know, a fountain is playing.

Machines of Movement

I was passing through a rather enclosed part of the
hall; its spaciousness not apparent owing to the large bulk
of the partitions enclosing various machines, when I passed
a small wooden doorway set into one of the partitions.
On the door was a plaque, printed black on white. It said:

INTERLOCKING MACHINE ROOM

On entering the room I found it to be full of giant
metal crabs.

Great struts of thin metal rod crisscross from ceiling to
floor, making it impossible to see very far into the room.
The very air shudders with the vibration of these
machines. Although the constructions vary considerably,
one from the other, a large number of them have the
same basic shape. Their nucleus is a mass of rods and
other interlocking members, and they stand about ten feet
high. The arrangement of these rods is infinitely complex.
At their apex they are thickly composed, and are sur-

rounded by other parts which join them and permit their motion. They branch out, and at floor level each machine covers a considerable area.

All of the legs of these machines are connected by free-moving joints to the legs of the other units, and a movement of one causes an adjustment to the position of the other. The whole room is in motion, and the machines twitch each other with an action that appears almost lascivious in nature.

A rod near me is moved by the action of a neighbor's leg. This movement is communicated at the top of the unit to another of the legs, and it, in turn, imparts motion to a machine further away. As these machines work, a constant metallic clattering fills the air, as if the room is filled with typewriters.

The machines are slick and oiled; their movement is smooth, but gives an impression of great nervousness. All over this chamber are various other parts, all of which seem affected in some way by the movement of the rods. On the wall, near me, is fixed a plaque with a jointed arm extending from it. Taut wires radiate from either extremity into the skeletal gray. One end is angled up, the other down. As the wire of the higher end is pulled by some motion in the mass of interlocking parts, the arm reverses its position jerkily.

Perhaps, a million years ago, these machines were constructed in a delicate static balance, a frozen wave; and with the locking of the final link in the circuit, the fixing of the last jointed leg against leg, the balance was tripped. A motion would have run its path, twisting and turning about the machines, splitting itself, dividing again, until today this movement still ran about the constructions, diffused and unpredictable. A million strands of current, still splitting. And perhaps the machines had been so carefully designed that in another million years all the currents would begin to amalgamate, becoming less and less complex, until they finally became two, meeting in opposition and deadlock, all movement ceasing.

The mind drowns among the interlocking machines. Perhaps the reason is in the similarity of this abstract maze to that pattern formed by the neural current. Perhaps these patterns of motion parallel too closely the patterns of electricity that we call personality, and the one is disturbed by the other. Conversely, perhaps the very existence of a human mind in the room causes little eddies and whirls in the motion of the machines.

I was unable to stay in the interlocking machine room for more than a minute or two before the psychological effects became more than I could bear.

The Clock

A large number of the machines in the hall are partitioned off by boards, so that one often feels that one is walking in a constricted space, and loses completely the feeling of immensity that one often experiences in the hall. It was in such a place that I found, set against one "wall," the mechanism of an enormous clock. It was all of shining brass, and it stood no less than ten feet high. It was facing the wall, the dial and hands (if, in fact, any such existed) being completely invisible. The clock was triangular in shape, and was supported by a framework of sturdy brass, front and back, that curved down to provide four feet. There was no plate at the back of the clock, its arbors being seated in strips of brass that curved in beautiful shapes from the main framework.

Despite the largeness of the clock, it was built to delicate proportions. The wheels were all narrow-rimmed, and the pallets that engaged the escape wheel were long and

curved, like the fingernails of a woman. It was as if the
mechanism of an ordinary domestic clock had been
magnified to a great degree; there was none of the solidity
and cumbersomeness of the turret clock here. I discovered
to my surprise that this clock was powered, as most
domestic clocks, by a spring. However, this spring was
immense, and must have exerted a tremendous pressure
to operate the mechanism.

Although the whole movement was surmounted by the
escape wheel and anchor, which perched on the apex of
the triangle, the pendulum was disproportionately short,
stretching down little more than six feet. The slow tick
of this enormous clock was lacking in the lower partials,
and as a consequence was not disturbing.

As the clock was so large, motion could be seen among
the wheels, which moved, each to a varying degree, with
each tick of the clock. This was a fascinating sight, and
I stayed watching the clock for a considerable period of
time.

I wish that I could have seen the clock illuminated by
strong morning sunlight from a window.

Machines of Death—1

There is darkness in this part of the hall. Stray light
illuminates black, pitted metal. I can see little of the
machine of death; it is to my right, and is a bleak high
wall of metal. The end of a thick chain extrudes here,
turns, and plunges back into the metal wall. The chain is a
foot wide and four inches thick. The only other feature
of this machine is a waste pipe which is sticking out from
the wall. Underneath this pipe is a channel set into the

floor, which conducts the waste to a nearby drain. The all-pervasive stink of this drain makes breathing difficult.

The pipe is pouring blood into the channel.

Machines of Death—2

This machine is very large, sprawling, and complicated. It appears to be completely functionless. It is possible that it was constructed to be entirely symbolic in nature, or alternatively that the things—creatures—upon which it operated are here no longer.

It consists of a vast network of girders, all of which are vibrating with a strange jogging motion. The only parts of the machine not affected by this movement are the two great supports at either end. The supports are each a framework of girders, and they contain various driving chains and gearing devices. At the top of each of these frames is a long jointed arm, of tremendous proportion. These arms also carry chains and gears. At the end of each arm is an enormous blade, made of a silver metal that catches the small amount of light. The blades have complete mobility, and appear to be fixed on the arms by some kind of ball joint.

The motion of the arms and the blades is difficult to observe in detail and even more difficult to describe. Analyzing the action in words tends to give an impression of slowness, when in fact, considering the bulk of the parts, it is very swift indeed.

The arms rest close to their supports, their joints extending downward like elbows, the blades upright. Keeping the blades in the same position, they move together across the thirty-yard space. When they are only about a yard apart, the arms are almost fully extended, and the motion stops for an instant. Then abruptly the blades begin to

move independently. They execute, in the space of only
a few seconds, a complicated system of movements—
thrusts, parries, arabesques—the motion of each blade
being the mirror of the other. Then again comes the pause,
and the arms bend again, carrying the blades back to
the supports.

The action of these blades certainly suggests physical
mutilation, and I found, as I watched, that I was wondering whether in fact the machine was still complete. Was
there once a feeding mechanism that carried the bodies
over to the knives to be sculptured within a few seconds to
a raw, twitching mass?

Despite the unpleasant feelings that the machine
arouses, I found it a fascinating experience to watch the
blades, and also the complex system of vibrating girders
beneath them. It is strange to see such large objects in
such rapid motion; the throbbing of the floor testified to
the weight of the mechanism, which must have been in
the hundreds of tons.

On the occasion that I observed the machine, there
were two other people there as well; a man and a woman.
At first I thought that they were part of the machine, but
my attention was caught by the fact that their own
vibrating motion was slightly lagging behind that of the
machine as their soft bodies absorbed their impetus.

They were both naked, and they were on one of the
girders directly below the high knives. The man was lying
on his back, stretched along the girder, and the woman
was squatting astride his hips. The jogging of the girder
was throwing their bodies up and down in a mechanical
travesty of copulation. The man was grasping the woman's
thighs tightly, and her face, turned toward me, with her
bottom lip between her teeth, was florid and beaded with
sweat. I could see her nostrils contracting with each gasped
breath she took.

A drop of oil fell from the knives as they clashed above,

and dropped unnoticed onto her shoulder. As it ran down
the pale flesh of her arm, it looked like a single drop of
ancient blood.

Machines of Death—3*

The machine sits in distance unheard. I walk on dry
sin, on the shit of us all, a man by my side who points
out all his bones. The well has now dried and all that
remains is a glowing, radioactive silt. The universe is
shaped like a whirlpool, and the vortex is here. Here is the
end of all time, the end of all space. The ultimate nil. I
have eaten my fill; here is my place; there is no single way
left to climb, and the rest is just fear. This cul-de-sac is
arid and death-cool. It is bleakness, a focus-point built
by man and his pains. The door must be tried; I pull and
it groans, and opens up wide. The chamber is small, but
light is let in to show me a word——
Auschwitz!

The Mother

This machine is standing in isolation; it is surrounded
by space on all sides. It is extremely large, standing almost
a hundred feet high, and it is shaped like an elongated
onion, tapering at the top to a high spire. From one side

* This machine consists of a flat surface of metal with a
circular metal door which leads to a small chamber, called the
"compressor," or "pot." Apart from this the wall is featureless
except for a switch by the side of the door. This area seems
to be the most dismal place in the entire hall.

of the machine, from about ten feet up, a flaccid rubbery
tube hangs down and outward to ground level.

The onion-belly of the Mother is completely featureless,
and light catches its curves; the tube is of a dull red
shade.

There are sounds coming from inside the metal body,
soft but constant. But then, abruptly, they stop, and all is
silent.

At the top of the tube, a bulge becomes apparent,
swelling outward all the time. Slowly, this bulge begins to
travel inside the tube, away from the machine and down
to the ground. While all this is going on, one obtains an
impression of supreme effort, and, strangely, pain. Perhaps
it is because the whole process is so slow. The object
creeping down the tube will eventually reach the end
and emerge into the light; one realizes this, and feels an
almost claustrophobic impatience with the slowness of
the event. There is a feeling too of compression and
relaxation, and one finds one's own muscles clenching in
time to the imagined contractions.

Eventually the bulge reaches the end of the tube at
ground level. This is where the real struggle begins. One
becomes aware that the end of the tube is beginning to
dilate, slowly and rhythmically. The belly of the machine
is as smooth and unevocative of any emotion as ever,
but it is impossible for the observer not to feel that agonies
are now being endured. One realizes that the process is
completely irreversible; that there is no way of forcing the
bulge back up the tube and inside the metal shell again.

Wider and wider grows the aperture at the end of the
tube, affording one an occasional glimpse of shiny moisture
within. A glint of metal is now and then apparent.

The tube dilates to its fullest extent, and a metal form
is suddenly revealed, covered in dripping brown fluid. The
rubber slides over its surface, releasing it more and more by

the second. Abruptly it bursts free in a wash of amniotic oil.

All is still.

The oil begins to drain away, and the new machine stands there motionlessly as the liquid drains from its surfaces. It is a small mechanism on caterpillar tracks, with various appendages at its front end which seem to be designed for working metal, or stone.

With a whirr, it jerks into action, and it moves softly away from the great Mother. There is a click from the parent machine, and the noises inside begin again.

I have watched this mechanism for long periods, and it appears to create only two kinds of machine. They are both on the same basic design, but one appears to be made for erection, the other for demolition.

The Mother has probably been working thus for hundreds of years.

Electronics

Electric machines stare at me with warm green eyes. I see nothing but bright plastic surfaces, inset with pieces of glass. These are still machines, active but unmoving, and in my ears is the faint hum of their life. The only movement here which indicates that the machines are in operation is the kicking of meters and the occasional jog of an empty tape spool.

Their function is not apparent; they work here at nameless tasks, performing them all with electronic precision and smoothness.

There are wires all over the room, and their bright, primary colors contrast strikingly with the overall pastel tones of the plastic bodies.

SONATA IN THE STYLE OF MACHINES

In a small chamber to the rear of the room of electric machines, there are some more of a different kind. The door to this small room is of wood, with a square glass set into it. The room appears to have remained undisturbed for many years.

They line three walls of the chamber, and are covered with switches and meters. They hum in strange configurations of sound, and appear to be making electric music together.

Death of Machines—1

In this part of the hall, all is still. Spiked mounds of time rise round me, their hulks encrusted with brown decay. The floor is totally covered by a soft carpet of rust, and its acrid odor stings the nostrils. A piece detaches itself from one of the tall machines and drifts to the floor, a flake of time. Many such flakes have fallen here in this part of the hall.

Time burns fire in my eyes, and I turn my head, looking for escape. But everywhere I see seconds and hours frozen into these red shapes. Here is a wheel, its rim completely eaten through; there a piston, its moveable parts now fixed in a mechanical *rigor mortis*. A reel of wire has been thrown into a corner, ages in the past, and all that remain are its circular traces in the dust.

My feet have left prints in the rust-carpet.

Death of Machines—2

I had come into the hall with my girl, and we had
spent a long time wandering about, hand in hand, when
we suddenly came on the remains of a machine.

It stood about six feet in height, and I could see that
at one time it had been of great complexity. For some
reason my girl was not very interested, and went off to see
something else, but I found that this particular machine
made me feel very sad. It appeared to be entirely composed of needles of metal, arranged in a thick pattern.
The largest of these needles was about three inches long,
and there appeared to be no way for the machine to hold
together. My guess is that when it was made, the needles
were fitted in such a way that the whole thing struck an
internal balance. The machine was now little more
than a gossamer web of rust; it must have had tremendous
stability to have remained standing for such a long time.

It was fascinating to look closely at its construction, to
see the red lines fitting together so densely. It was like
looking into a labyrinth; a system of blood-red caves.
With every movement of my head a whole new landscape
was presented to me. I called my girl over, and we stood
hand in hand, looking at the dead machine.

I think that it must have been our body heat, for
neither of us made an excessive movement, but at that
moment the entire construction creaked, and sank a few
inches. Then there was a sigh, and the whole thing dissolved into dust about our feet.

Both of us felt very subdued when we left the hall.

*I hope that the above information has enabled my read-
ers to gain an impression of this very exciting hall. There
is little that I can add, except the following point.*

You will remember from one of the accounts I have

printed here, the one giving details of the creation of new machines, the following passages: "It is a small mechanism on caterpillar tracks, with various appendages at its front end which seem to be designed for working metal, or stone." ". . . it appears to create only two kinds of machine . . . one appears to be made for erection, the other for demolition." These two passages, together with some other material that I have not published here suggest an interesting point.

I believe that the machines mentioned are the same as those described in another account, in which the writer stood by one of the outer walls of the hall. He watched one set of machines building a wall about six inches further out than the old one, which was being torn down by the other mechanisms. This seems to be a process which is going on all the time, all over the hall; a new wall is built, slightly further out, and this in its turn will be demolished as another is put up.

I believe that the hall has been, from the time of its creation and always will be, increasing in size!

However, only more research will be able to establish this radical idea as an incontrovertible fact.

THE COMING OF THE SUN

CELLAR FIRE

Rudolf opened the cellar door, spilling light into the dim chamber. He walked carefully down the wooden steps, the yellow light shining on his bald scalp. He coughed as fumes from the dormant paraffin-fired boiler caught at his throat, and as he reached the bottom of the steps he muttered slow obscenities.

Normally Michael would come down here with him to supervise this preparing of the boiler, but Michael couldn't make it this time. He was in the hospital after being attacked by someone. Rudolf smiled to himself and a silver line coursed down his chin.

Rudolf was tall, but stooped. All his movements were slow and deliberate and accompanied by gruntings and pantings as if each one cost him supreme effort or pleasure. A pink scar traced a smooth curve over the surface of his shaven head, as if following the sutures of the skull beneath. He was dressed in a formless garment of rough gray cloth. In his mind there was very little, save for a general hatred of a world that had done him some unspecified wrong. His hatred was generalized, directed toward tables, chairs, walls, as well as people.

His life was here. His past was now far buried, and his half-formed thoughts swirled about his skull like mist rising on a marsh.

He shuffled across the room to the cans of paraffin. "Bastards . . ." he muttered to the cans, as he bent to pick one up. If he was capable of liking any place, then he liked it here in the cellar. He liked the wet brick walls,

the dark corners; he liked the cobwebs and the wooden
boxes stacked in the far corner; he liked the silence and
the electric light bulb which swung on its flex, swaying the
room back and forth beneath his feet. He liked the smells
of the cellar, the smells of mustiness and decay.

He moved to the boiler with his can of paraffin swaying
in his hand, and lowered the can to the floor. He
unscrewed the fuel cap on the pump and inserted the
funnel. Bending down slowly, he lifted and tilted the can,
watching the blue liquid bubbling down the vortex of
the funnel. When the can was empty he threw it, smiling,
into the corner, enjoying the clanging sound it made.
Michael wouldn't have allowed him to throw the can. He
primed the boiler, and when the pressure was up, pressed
the green button. A glow came to life behind a small
square of glass and a chugging sound began. There was a
flash, a bang, and the boiler fired, a jet of flame appearing
behind the glass. He enjoyed looking at the fire; that was
why he had come down here without supervision, to
press his nose, as he was doing now, against the glass and
to watch the potent flare jetting and roaring.

After a while he became tired of looking at the flame,
and turned once again to the collection of cans in the
corner. He shuffled across, his ragged clothes trailing on
the dirty floor. He unscrewed the cap of one of the cans,
and drew in, his nose pressed into the can, the oily softness
of the paraffin's odor. Then he raised the can slowly above
his head, in both hands, and inverted it so that the liquid
fell in a broken stream, splashing on to the floor, soaking
the bottoms of his trouser legs. He felt an unusual
excitement, and breathed in deeply.

When the can was empty, the floor was swimming with
liquid. He looked at the other cans; they reminded him
of policemen. He didn't like policemen; a vague freak of
memory told him that policemen didn't believe in Jesus.
He went to the other cans and, one by one, he twisted off
the caps, and threw them about the room. There were

about thirty cans, and they stood at his feet, their round
mouths open in surprise. He was like a king, and they
stood at his feet like subjects. He felt happy.

He kicked at them, and one fell over, bubbling away
its life.

"Bastards. . . ."

He picked up one of the cans and swung it round,
creating a transient parabola of blueness that sparkled in
the light and then sprayed both him and the room. His
skull was throbbing, and something began to grow in his
throat; he had to gasp for breath. His big hands clenched
and unclenched at his sides, and the breath whistled
through his teeth. He picked up another of the cans, held
it upside-down and deliberately sprayed his feet. He
threw its corpse away, and as it bounced into the corner
shouted, "Clatter!"

He had no memory of feeling like this before. Actually
he had, many times in childhood, and he had last felt it
in a woodyard between the thighs of an anonymous
woman.

He picked up another can, emptied and killed it, and
threw it away. Another. Another. He strode among the
cans, kicking, pushing aside, growing in stature all the
time. The smell of paraffin was strong in the air now, and
he gloried in the odor, filling his chest with its stickiness.

When all the cans had been emptied, he stood with
his feet in the paraffin, beating his chest with a large hand,
his scar bright red and appearing to glow in the dim cellar
light.

An idea began to grow in his mind. He found that he
was shaking with excitement. A stirring began in his groin,
and he put out long and clumsy arms, wanting to
embrace anything. He walked over to the boiler and
picked up a metal rod that had been standing nearby. His
throat was nearly blocked now, and his body was constantly shaken by small shudders.

He plunged down the rod and smashed the thick glass. The flame was free, to breathe!

For a while he watched the flame, smiling at it, then he abruptly bent down and ripped a strip of cloth from his trouser leg. He dipped it into the paraffin until it was soaked. He suddenly found tears filling his eyes. He lowered the cloth on to the roaring flame, and through the tears saw it burst with dancing fire that was reflected a million times to become a universe of light.

He wiped his eyes and, while he could still see, threw the flaming cloth into the center of the floor. For a while, nothing happened, but suddenly the fire widened and widened, from a drop, to a pool, to a lake, to a sea of fire. He felt a rising and a swelling, and as the fire grew, so did he. Fumes were in the air, and the cellar was lit with a brightness that it had never known before. It was hot, and as the fire came closer to him, hotter.

At the end he stood there, arms and legs outstretched, erect and potent, shouting with happiness at the flame, his friend and creation.

Finally he knew the glorious pain of self-immolation.

IN THE LOUNGE

Light comes through the french windows and splashes warmly across the parquet floor, reflecting into the far corners of the room. Near the window is a grand piano, and a man sits at it, dressed in rough gray clothing. On his face is a look of complete involvement in what he is playing; his eyes are half-closed and he sways his head from side to side. His hands rise and fall, jerkily and mechanically, and he plays a constant series of random and dissonant chords.

Also in the room, sitting in armchairs facing each other, are two people: a man and a woman.

JOHN: Are you sure you feel all right this morning, Mary?

MARY: Yes thanks, John, fine; it's just that poor Robert sitting there makes me feel a bit depressed. (They both glance at the pianist.)

JOHN (to the pianist): Good morning, Eusebius!

PIANIST (turning quickly and speaking swiftly and angrily): *Florestan!*

MARY (shivering): Oh! I hate this place!

JOHN: Well, I don't think you're alone in that. I think we all hate it—even the ones who don't know anything.

MARY: Yes. So many of them don't understand, but you can sense that they feel fear, just the same as us. (She glances at the piano again.)
One, two, three, four. . . . I wonder how many chords he plays each day? I wonder whether he enjoys it, or whether each note is a torment.

JOHN: And there's Colin, every day, curled up in the bathroom, his hairy legs in front of him like a trembling shield. It's like living constantly in some kind of disaster area.

MARY: Yes, a moment after the disaster has occurred; there is the same feeling here of mute horror, just like the first few seconds after an accident.

JOHN: The Hindenberg falls in smoking ruins by breakfast time; at lunch the Titanic meets its end, and Christ is crucified by dinner time.

MARY: Oh, I wish I could *leave!*

JOHN: How can we? There's no way out for us past the eyes of authority. Two mistakes have been made, we are forgotten, and here we shall remain until we're too old to care any more. . . .

MARY: Oh, please don't! The whole thing depresses me so much. Let's go out somewhere; would you like a walk in the garden?

JOHN (preoccupied): Yes . . . yes . . . in a while.
(MARY suddenly inclines her head and sniffs at the air.)

MARY: John—can you smell something?

JOHN (vaguely): What?

MARY: It's almost . . . as if something's . . . burning.

JOHN: I saw . . . two dogs once . . .

MARY: John—I'm sure there's something burning! I
think we should get out!

JOHN: . . . two dogs in the street . . .

MARY: Perhaps it's just a bonfire.

JOHN: . . . not doing anybody any harm. . . .

A SCENE IN THE STREET

The scene is a medium-sized suburban shopping center. Fairly heavy traffic is moving past, but there are not
many people on the pavements. Outside one of the shops,
a grocer's, the shopkeeper is talking to two women shop-
pers.

There are two dogs padding about the pavement,
sniffing each other. The shopkeeper looks disapprovingly
at the dogs, and then turns his bright attention back to
the women. One of the dogs makes an attempt to mount
the other, but then drops back to all fours again, and they
continue to move about from one side of the pavement to
the other.

The grocer is a tall man, and he prides himself on his
friendliness toward his customers. He had a hard time
when he was younger, trying to establish himself, but now
he is the owner of a thriving shop, and is able to spare
the time to chat to his young housewives. Also he is not
sure about one of the women to whom he is talking. She
has only been here for a short time, and she seems to be
exceptionally friendly. He wonders if, one day, she might
be good for a turn. He is beginning to develop a paunch,
but is rather proud of it, and likes to rest his hands on it.

The smaller of the dogs again mounts the other, and
they begin to copulate there on the pavement. The grocer
and the housewives see this copulation out of the corners
of their eyes, but the housewives carry on talking brightly.

The grocer, however, is annoyed. He sees the behavior of the dogs as an annoyance, almost as an insult. The ladies are, for a moment, talking to each other.

The grocer seizes his opportunity, walks over, and gives the dogs a kick.

However, his boot strikes only the male dog. The animal is spun round so that he is facing away from the female, but is still in her. As the grocer walks back, the dog screams in agony. Its twisted penis is still congested with blood, which now cannot escape. A permanent erection now binds him fast to the female in an agonizing union. The female dog is frightened and begins to run, dragging the male backwards.

The grocer and the ladies, embarrassed, try not to notice, and carry on their conversation.

The screams of the trapped dog become even more pitiful as the creature is dragged away swiftly by the female. The level of sound in the street drops as people become aware of the suffering dogs. People turn to watch as the creatures disappear down the street.

The grocer is very embarrassed, and more than a little angry.

IN THE COURTYARD

He found himself alone in a dark courtyard. He had been there for a long, long time. He remembered sunlight and contentment, but now his world was filled with his desire for escape.

To his right, curving down to the dark tarmac of the yard was a wind vent, its black throat yawning in air noisily. It was a silver structure, square in outline, and he kept away from its mouth. The yard was in shadow, made even blacker by the sunlight above. The sun never reached down here. On three sides black buildings rose in the air, and loomed beside and behind him, but on the fourth, a long way above, sunlight broke across the wall like glass, and splintered a rude balcony with light. At

the balcony was a door, and he knew that behind the door
was a small chamber, big enough to accommodate the
small staircase that led through the manhole to the grassy
field above.

All around the courtyard were the corpses of small
animals, and in the far corner lay a crazed donkey, a silver
spoon buried in its neck, ready for someone to come along
to scoop out a mouthful of melting flesh. All about the
donkey were flies, feeding off its craziness, and it gave to
the world its fetid odor without shame or pride.

Fire escapes jutted blackly above him. He clawed back
the life bulging in his throat. A shaft of black brick, a
basic buttress, sloped from one side of the courtyard to
the other. In this enclosed place it was like a beam from
some black and dusty sun. He leaned against a wall, and
brick crumbled under his twitching fingers. In front of
him was a steel ladder that reached up to the balcony, but
he was scared to climb. There was everything to lose.

But now the odor of burning oil reached his nostrils,
and fear for his life came to him. He must leave!

He grasped the rungs of the ladder and began to climb.
But he could not; his feet would not respond to him. He
fell back, almost screaming.

There was a movement above him on the balcony. It
was a slim Jewish girl. She was shouting something down
to him, but he couldn't hear what she was saying.

"I can't hear you!" he called, but she indicated her
ears and shook her head sadly. He realized that she was
deaf. She reached down to him with an imploring
expression on her face. He realized what he must do. He
began to climb the ladder again, but found it now a little
easier. As he climbed toward her, so she strained her
hands down to him. As their flesh closed in contact he felt
a wild crackling strength coursing into him. He climbed
over the railing and on to the balcony, she helping him.
Once over, he stood and looked into her large, dark eyes,
still holding her hands.

"You saved me," he said.

"No, you helped me as well. And I haven't saved you; you can't beat geometry."

"I couldn't hear you, down there."

"I know. I've been in a very similar place."

He looked back over his shoulder. The yard, from up here, was much smaller than he remembered it. The donkey, far below, twitched his tail with mad contempt.

"I shall never go back there," he said. "And I shall never leave you."

She smiled. "You will. The answer is written in the very curves of space, the geometry of time. Kiss me."

The power from her was welling through him, and his body floated with the breeze that blew about. He took her in his arms, and pressed his lips gently against hers. She was warm in his arms and his mouth; he closed his eyes, and let his body sing the song they had begun.

And then she was gone.

There was nothing. He turned wildly, his arms flailing the air. As he turned he slipped, and fell back into the yard. But he fell slowly, descending like a feather into darkness. He sprawled on the cold tarmac, sobbing into the dust.

He got up on his knees and stared at the balcony which swam in his gaze. There was another woman there, and as he watched her hair changed color, her features flowed like treacle into new combinations of line and form. Sometimes she seemed old, sometimes she was young and fresh. Each time she reached down to him, but he could not hear what she was saying; he couldn't reach up to touch her hands. Sometimes she was too weak to lift him; sometimes she just looked at the sky; sometimes she reached for someone else whom he could not see. Once she was sad and beautiful, and he rushed for the ladder, but she didn't see him, and was lost in contemplation of of her own feet.

"I remember a neater arrangement than this!" he called to her.

Time danced like fireflies across his brow. He sensed the years falling, brown skeletal leaves of age, and he put out his hand to brush them as they fell.

And all the time he could feel the ground shaking and the angry fire nearing him for its revenge. . . .

Finally her features changed again. Above him stood a girl with blue eyes and with pale musicians moving in a procession through her mind.

"Help me!" he called to her. "I NEED YOU!" just realizing that he did.

Her mouth began to move anxiously, but a second after her lips moved, a cracked voice spoke a foreign tongue into his ears. The sounds she made brought agony to him.

"Go!" he shouted. "Go away!" He ran to the other side of the courtyard to escape the pain she was causing him. She began to grow transparent, fading into nothing. Just before she disappeared he realized that he could understand what she was saying.

But now all was bright; the fire was coming to claim him.

IN THE LOUNGE

All is unchanged. JOHN and MARY still sit in their facing chairs. ROBERT still plays the piano like an automaton. There is a strong smell of smoke in the air.

JOHN: The strange thing about this place is that no one really knows anything about anybody else. None of us has a past life. We are all here, living in the immediate present with nothing at all behind us. Perhaps we were all created here; perhaps there is nothing outside at all. Perhaps this whole place is the only thing in the universe, and that what we see from our windows is nothing but a backdrop painted to deceive us. I often

worry about this, you know. In fact the other day I put
my arm through the bars over my window, right up
to the shoulder, but I didn't touch anything.

MARY: I had a terrible dream last night.

JOHN: Mary—I'm sure I can smell smoke.

MARY: I dreamed I had a husband. . . . I dreamed a past life
for myself.

JOHN: I'll swear there's something on fire.

MARY: I dreamed a complete past. . . . I dreamed love and
pain and death and friends and enemies.

JOHN: I think we should see what is burning.

MARY: I dreamed that I fed from my husband. When he
loved me I would draw sweetness and strength from his
body. He would enter my body with his, and my soul
with his. He would move inside me, shaking me,
and my body would respond, and twist and turn to
receive the power and the love of him. This was my
dream: He is loving me. *This is me!* I feel, *this respon-
sive, mindless creature is me! Everything else is false.* I
cling to him, my fingers pressing into his back. My
head is moving from side to side, but all I can feel is him
in me and my body responding to his power. He
penetrates my bowels, my chest, my eyes; he is everywhere in me, there is nothing but him. I call his name
out into the world, but the world is him, and he is
moving in me. Our bodies stiffen in one. I strain up to
him, and his body gasps rigidly down to me. And then
there is nothing but the soundless explosion to which I
abandon myself.

  And then we are both quiet. His face is on the pillow
by my shoulder, and his weight presses me down.

  I didn't tell you about my husband, did I? He is a
very big man. When he was younger, he was powerful
and muscled. He is still strong, but now the flesh of
middle age swells his belly. He is heavy on me as we
lie there, but I do not care. Nothing matters but the

strength I have drawn from him. He is quieter than
usual, and so am I. I lie, staring up peacefully at the
ceiling, illuminated by the bedside light. I stroke
his shoulder, and decide eventually that he has gone to
sleep. I will give him a few minutes before I wake him.
His weight is now uncomfortable, but I vow to
endure it for a while until I am forced to disturb him.
(MARY's voice is gradually getting higher, and a light of
hysteria is coming into her eyes.)

His shoulders feel cold, and I pull up the blankets to
cover them. And then . . . and then I try to wake him.
I push his shoulder gently, but he does not wake. I
smile indulgently, and push again a little harder. The
flesh gives under my hand, but he does not respond. I
call his name . . . again . . . and then I smell it. The
smell of death.
(The last part of MARY's story is screamed out.)

I smelt the death of him in that bed. Have you ever
read in the papers, "He died in his sleep"? I was
pinned under him. I tried desperately to get him away
from me. I hit his shoulder again and again, but I
could not get a response from him. I tried to escape
from under him . . . he was still in me . . . but I could
not. I cried and screamed and tried to force life back
in. I held his face up, and saw his dead eyes. His eyes
stared at me like a dead fish's eyes. His face was
distorted in a terrible twisted smile.

I tried to push his head away, but it fell back on to
my shoulder, giving me a dead man's kiss—cold saliva
on my flesh. I remember that I felt now nothing but a
terrible revulsion for him. I must try to escape. . . .
I must unjoin myself from him. I remember that I
twisted and turned, moving my hips as if I were loving
this crushing body. I strained myself, careless of myself,
saying something, I forget what. And at last his dead
prick no longer touched my body. I couldn't get from
underneath him. . . . I put my hands under his corpse

and tried to lift it off . . . but even with the strength of
panic I couldn't do it. Time went past. His flesh cooled.
I cursed him, I jerked and twitched under him. . . . I
remember spittle drooling all over my face, and I
remember calling and crying and punching and groaning
. . . but his weight pinned me flat on the bed. And I
remember that at last someone heard my screams and
came . . . and they brought me here! HERE! THEY
BROUGHT ME HERE!
(MARY begins to scream and writhe in her chair. JOHN
is not looking at her, but is talking quietly to himself.
The pianist continues to play his chords.)

THE BURNING CLOCK

It is an American wall clock. Its case is made of wood,
square, with two supporting columns that rise from the
bottom to the top. A large arch of glass is in front, and two
side panels form gothic curves. The face and mechanism
is supported behind the front arch, at the top, and the
pendulum, with a large, flat brass bob, hangs almost to the
bottom of the case.

Flames have just caught at the bottom of the case, and
the watching man leans closer to see better. The wood at
the bottom of the right-hand column is beginning to char.
The flames have caught quickly, and begin to reach up the
sides of the clock. The fire also burns at the base of the
clock, and a discolored patch can be seen on the "floor"
through the front glass. He looks at the burning column on
the right. Varnish has peeled off all the way up, and the
whole column is now burning fiercely. There is a crack, and
the side glass splinters. The back of the clock has now
caught fire.

Suddenly a flame appears inside the clock, as the baseboard burns completely through. The flames engulf the
pendulum bob as it swings gently to and fro. Now flames
are rising inside the clock and, for a while, the clock

resembles a glass case of fire. Then the fire outside the clock
gains a better hold, and abruptly the front glass cracks.
Half of the glass falls to the floor and shatters; the other
half clings to the blackening wood. Now the bob can only
be seen as it emerges from the fire at the extreme ends of
its swing; it can be seen now that parts of the pendulum
are glowing red. Although the hands, which he can just
distinguish in the flare, are not pointing to the hour or
the half, the clock begins to strike. The clock strikes twelve,
and then goes on.

The baseboard falls to the floor, trailing smoke behind
it, and smoulders there. The striking of the clock is
becoming erratic; the strokes are irregular, and slowing.
The front part of the clock swings open on its hinges, the
warping of the frame freeing it, and the remainder of the
glass crashes down. The flames are concentrated at the top
of the clock now; the pendulum is a glowing shaft of red.
The clock's striking mechanism seizes, and the sound
stops. The pendulum is now moving under its own
momentum, and its arc is diminishing; the clock is now
like a burning skeleton.

Metal drips down from the interior of the clock
mechanism in bright, hurried drops. The clock is now
completely still, only the flames dancing over its surface. He
moves round to the side of the clock, and sees its cogs,
warped and glowing. The sight disturbs him. It is as if the
flames are the only moving things in a petrified universe.
Great calcified images loom in his mind, and he presses the
back of his hand to his teeth to subdue his fear.

But then he sees that the clock has not burned at all;
it is just that the intense heat has caused it to stop.

THREE CATATONIC STORIES

A man runs across the room, fear glinting in his eyes. In
the corner, curled up like a slug, is the naked body of a man

called Colin. Beside him is a sheet of paper. The man picks
up the paper and reads:

1. A man is sitting at a table. The surface in front of him
is supporting a large block of gold, on a red silk cushion.
Lying on the table beside the nugget is a sharp silver
knife. The man licks his lips and rolls up his sleeves with
delicacy. Then he puts out his hands, grasping the knife
with one and holding the block with thumb and forefinger
of the other. The gold is pure, and much softer than gold
usually is. Its outside surface has a dull gleam. The man
picks up the knife, and brings it deliberately to a point
above the block. He lowers it to the dull golden surface and
carefully draws it across, scoring a straight bright line across
the top. For a few seconds he holds the knife poised,
regarding his work critically. Then he brings down the
knife again and draws it across once more, but this time
with more pressure, slicing through the gold as if it were
butter and exposing the bright gleam of its inner surface.

He neatly bisects the block, and, with the knife, moves
the two pieces apart. This is the moment of consummation.
A few heavy seconds pass. Then he puts down the knife,
with gold adhering to its blade, and picks up one of the
sections of the golden block. His lips are full and wet;
he parts them and pushes in the gold. He licks the moist
gold from his fingers.
FIRE
2. There is a plain. It is dark in color and absolutely
flat, like the polished top of a table. There is an impression
of depth about the plain, and it gleams faintly.

In the center of the plain, standing like a passion
translated into stone, is a cathedral. At this distance the
cathedral cannot be seen in detail, but its general shape, the
light on its windows, can just be made out.

A man is riding a motorcycle across the plain, at high
speed. The plain is intensely cold, and the temperature

is dropping by the minute. The man is trying to reach the
cathedral before the cold is enough to cause his consciousness to fail and make him plunge to the ground. The
roar of his engine echoes from unseen obstacles. He
rockets across the ground, nearing the cathedral swiftly.
Soon the shape of the building is towering over him, and he
throttles down, gradually slowing. He overshoots the
cathedral and circles it, its features flashing past him in a
jumble of gray stonework.

On his second circuit he turns in and travels through
the door, right into the nave. Inside, the cathedral is very
spacious and warm. Light comes in and makes the stone
warm and sensual with its stained-glass colors. About
three-quarters down the cathedral nave is the altar. The rest
of the floor space is empty, save for a few benches cluttered
in the center.

The man turns his motorcycle to the right, and travels
slowly down one side of the nave. The sound of the engine
comes booming back at him from the high roof. He circles
the nave, the light turning his flesh into a shifting sequence
of color and texture. As he twists the throttle control his
engine noise becomes higher and rises to a recognizable
note. The engine backfires, and the tremendous report
echoes into a continuous sound. The stonework throws back
throbbing reflections of the engine noise; it is as if all
the sound he has made since entering the door is still
winging about from one side of the building to the other.
The air brushes his face, and he speeds up, dipping his
machine at the corners. The note of his engine rises still
more.

And abruptly there is something else in the air. A dis-
turbance shudders in the nave. A response—a conflict.
Still faster he travels, flinging his motorcycle round the
nave. The note of the engine rises in a roar.

And suddenly he has it.

His engine note hits one of the harmonics of the basic

resonance frequency of the cathedral, and all the air in the building begins to vibrate in a sympathetic resonance.

As he speeds round, he coaxes the sound from the depths. The air shudders deeply, louder and louder, until the cathedral-note has been completely evoked, and the deep shuddering is almost unbearable. Now he knows he will never leave the cathedral. As he cycles round, holding the throttle steady, he begins to laugh, an activity that is noiseless in the great mass of vibrating air, his motorcycle sound lost in the giant organ note of the building.

On the plain, the cathedral sounds.

FIRE BRIGHT

3. A man is born, whose body is constructed in such a way that positive space exerts a tremendous pressure on his cellular structure. He may only obtain a lessening of these sensations by standing in front of large mirrors, when positive space is balanced to a degree by the residual pressure from negative space. By placing two mirrors, one each side of him, both facing inward, the balancing of tensions affords him exquisite relief.

One day the pressures become intolerable, and he tries to escape them by leaping into a full-length mirror. He becomes trapped, merged with his "negative" image. He is forced to hang motionless, caught in the interstices of positive and negative space, at the point where the two intersect. He doesn't have the strength to move himself; the power-weight ratio permits him only to move one finger. This he does often, projecting it into normal or negative space, but each time the finger is two-dimensional, and the stresses are immense.

He hangs, trapped in a glacier of force.

FIRE BURN BRIGHT

The man puts down the paper and turns to the fetus beside him, but now in his eyes there is an expression of lost despair. He speaks without conviction. "You must

come with me—we must escape." The door at the end of
the room blossoms into orange light. ". . . must come with
me . . ." says the fetus, ". . . must escape . . ." A faint hint
of urgency and panic comes into the man's voice. "Come
. . . quickly!" "Come . . . quickly!" Tongues roar into the
room. The man turns, ignoring the hunched form on the
floor, and begins to scream, in a high, childish voice. He
drops to his hands and knees and begins to wail like a baby,
beating his fists on the parquet flooring. It is very warm
in the room.

BLACK WAVE, TAKE ME AWAY WITH YOU

Flat and polished tables of black glass—head of flutes
shrilling like Cocteau's opium pipes—wide gray façade
"Charing Cross Hotel" through rain going in distance and
past—sun drips blood into a sea of tears making the green
one red . . . weave your bandages of gold—flat façade, wide
and gray filled out with deperspectived spaces—bully
shouldered perverts take each other sexually, and us—men
sob in the lavatory—paraschizophrenic moves walls and
time by psychokinesis—Eusebius plucks dead chords from
the piano, crying—the walls weep with memories of you—
timemen lurk round corners waiting for more time to
destroy—locked in the washroom, naked people cry out as
ice-water jets their flesh, fiercely—dirty old men communicate telepathically with God—my own legs tremble
before me with beautiful fear—rimed with blue glory
they await the coming of the sun. . . .

Smoke comes from the sky like a scent of lemons—I am
coming—I am coming. . . .

SOLEIL DE SANG, D'OISEAUX

It is quiet in this house behind my windows
My Jesus, my universe of silence and bells
There is only more windows; layers of glass

Throw to me the lance of love, my Love
And I can look out through the layers of glass
Make of yourself a cauldron for my heart
See the slow flower-garden and the ghosts of love

Give me the red and the green of your love
Inside this house it is very quiet
Rainbow of love, desert of love
Like a cave and I am here
Your golden pillars are singing to me
I am here in a cave in a house behind glass

They slowly swing, the bells of the depths
And I am falling apart and dying
Do not wake me: it is the time of the bird!

EVENTS IN HELL

Time sinks wells into my brain—sutures hum with
electrical circuits—Russian death machines swing wide
barrels and project electrical rays into my eyes—faces, fatty,
broken, and degenerate strain at the sun's glory—fantasies
of life crackle among dendrides—an old man masturbates
his death-tool and spits white glory at the sun—morons
concentrate on the intellectual promise of a piece of wood
—my head is a gramophone horn sounding music-hall songs
out to the stars.

DEAD BOOK IMAGES SPIN IN MY MIND LIKE SNOW

Book jackets fall spinning to my floor—God rises in me
like a vapor from snow—the sound of my voice echoes in
levels of light—a rainbow of love to the vision of your face
—Give me the thirst of your love; the tumescence of your
love.
Motorcycles ride across the plain of snow—black

mosquito squadrons of desire—The snow lies on my soul
like the seal of your name—Send your motorcycles to me—
Give me the red and the green of your love—my man, my
woman, my child, my God.

Levels of consciousness hide your bells in light—Sound
waves of glory put my soul to flight—The sun of blood
is trembling on the bleeding snow—The colors of your love
flux in a brilliant flow—Your core of acquiescence swells
in me—Dead images are floating on the sea.

Book jackets are trampled by jack boots—a dead web
stretches across the swelling surfaces of dead water—the
smiling, deep surfaces—they welcome the laxness of
my new body—they hide their bowels in night—they
clasp soft hands under me and receive my weakness—I see
your light far above me, your sun, your blood—but I feel
the warmth of their embrace, the kiss of their foul water-
skin touches my lips—Your snow is burying me, and
your sun is burning my flesh—My ears are blinded by the
melody of your light—Their web is enfolding me, and I
can't escape its mesh—My body is sighing in a velvet field
of white—I am dying for you—your bells, your colors,
your heart—your heart is red and it pulses like the sun—
the clangor of your sunlight strikes my eyes like metal—
book images stir dust in my brain—I die for your colors,
your name.

CATATONIC SUN, FILL MY VALLEYS

Sun-mist, you are in me
Sun-fire, my fetus fills me with heat
Sun-death, your touch rests on my body
Sun, you are drying my leaves—my foliage moves under
    your hand
Sun, you are piercing my womb
Sun, my mouth is full of you
Sun, you are burning away my heart

RED PIANO

Across the room the red piano is playing—piano of pain
—Florestan plays desert chords, and the flame-piano
answers with cracks like a cannon. Strings curl over him
like a benediction.

THIS IS SUN

This is sun
Sun is blood
And the bone, gouged and crackling
Sun is the laughing of a pretty woman
And the voice of a great multitude
Sun is semen
Ejaculated in a spurt of blood
Sun is dust and the memory of old wounds
Sun is water in the softness of flood
Sun of the waters, here am I
I await you
This is Sun

SUN!

We are here sun sun glorious we wait for your rays
to lick us with tongues sun we call on you bring
your anger to bear on our flesh clean us with
your venom sun magic sun-spear of deadly passion
sun take us in to your burning embrace sun potent
sun glorious to join sun sun sun for the end of
burning the concerted rush to your condensed
sun-energy bloom for us sun unfold sun like a
glowing rose and wrap up in your burning petals. . . .

AHHH! PRAY

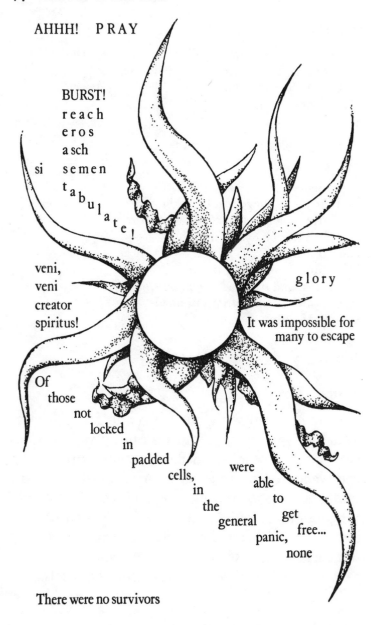

BURST!
r e a c h
e r o s
a sch
si s e m e n
t a b u l a t e !

veni,
veni   g l o r y
creator
spiritus!   It was impossible for
                              many to escape

Of
    those
        not
            locked
                in
                    padded
                        cells,   were
                            in   able
                                the   to
                                    general   get
                                        panic,   free...
                                            none

There were no survivors

THE EYE OF THE LENS

THE FILM

The film is shot on Agfacolour 16 mm. stock on a Bell &
Howell camera. It is shot at 24 frames per second, and
lasts for fifteen minutes, thirty-two seconds. The film has
an optical sound track, and is ideally projected with a screen
width of eight feet.

At certain points in the film color filters have been
used. The filters are very light, and serve only to give a
predominance to a particular color, rather than the effect
of a dense wash. At other points the same effect is achieved
by the selection of particular objects in the field of vision.
Thus objects of the chosen color appear on the screen
either isolated or as predominant elements.

THE CAST

A girl.
A florist.
A holy man.
Throughout the film, the girl wears a white, pleated
dress, caught at the waist by a length of gold chain, the
end of which hangs down her thigh.

She is slender, and moves with a light grace. Her hair is
long and dark; it is parted at the center, drawn back,
and hangs down between her shoulder blades. Her neck is
long, and her face has, despite its appearance of fragility, a
strong bone structure. In bare feet she stands at five feet
seven, and she has brown eyes.

Her teeth have been extensively filled, and when she
laughs one may see the glint of silver in her mouth. Her

body hair is rather slight, and on her legs there is an almost
invisible covering of sparse, dark hair. She sometimes tries
to be cool and off-hand, but she never succeeds with any
conviction.

Her skin is more brown than one would expect of a girl
with such a delicate appearance, but at her neck one is
able to see traceries of veins beneath the skin. Although she
has a nervous temperament, she is capable of deep serenity
and objectivity, and this is the mood she most often
projects throughout the film.

She is deeply ashamed of her breasts, slight, with long,
light nipples. Without realizing that this would spoil the
proportions of her body, she feels that her breasts should be
much larger than they are. This shame diffuses over her
whole being, and she is quite genuinely convinced that
she is rather unpleasantly ugly.

The florist and the holy man are played by the same
actor. In the case of the holy man, he wears a short russet
beard.

There is a large cast of extras, and the voice on the sound
track is that of a man.

THE IMAGES

The sound track is silent, save for the hissing that comes
through the loudspeakers. The screen is dark. Fade in. The
girl enters from the left. She walks ankle-deep through a
forest of broken icons. Gods with upturned faces, blind
eyes staring heavenward. Arms are broken off and stretch up
from the sea of figures, hands stretching out in supplicant
tension. The sun shines brightly, and casts deep shadows
among the bodies of the figurines. The screen is in parts
intolerably bright and absolutely black.
SOUND TRACK: "Love me red—love me green—my serenity
of soul fills all the places of earth—it calms the tempest
and quietens the wild beast.

"Love me red with bloody arrows and anoint my feet

with oil—let me plunge my arms into your wounds and
cleanse myself in the bubbling red stream. Give me the red
of your tortured eyes, the red of your bloody limbs—I
will take the red and build it into strength for my arms—
into wrath to fight the hatred of my life.

"Love me green—green of palm-leaf, of glory, that I
might some day rise to your feet and sing praises to your
name.

"Love me gold—gold of riches, that I might spread
your word throughout the land—that I might raise temples
in your name and spread your teachings to the ends of the
earth.

"Love me brown—the brown of leather, that I might
fashion whips for my flesh—to suffer the mortification
of your love—to live in the glory of fearful pain to the end
of my days.

"Give me all the colors of your being, that I might form
them into the pure white of resurrection and eternal life."

The girl clearly has been hearing the voice on the
sound track, and she stands for a moment, looking reflec-
tive, and then moves on. She passes out of the frame,
kicking the statuettes idly as she walks. The picture remains
for a few seconds, the idols looking, in the strong sunlight,
like a field of motionless gray corn.

Fade out, with a silent sound track.

THE SANDSTONE BUST

The girl is walking through the desert. The sand is lit
brightly by the sun, almost white, and her footprints are
softened by the shifting of the sand. The rounded contours
of the desert stretch to the horizon.

She passes an upturned bicycle, half buried in sand, like
the bones of a graceful creature. Its front wheel is
twisted toward her, and as she passes it appears to be
watching her with little interest and with patience born of
decay. She goes past the bicycle at a considerable distance.

The camera lifts as she passes, and the helicopter comes into view, its belly sunk deep into the sand. The fractured vanes move slightly in the breeze. Although, apart from this corpse-like movement, the helicopter is quite still, the canted mechanism appears as if it is trying to struggle up from the sand to fly away. It is like a photograph of a wounded creature. It is almost as though the film has seized in the projector, and if it started again the helicopter would hump and flap dreadfully on the desert sand.

The girl looks at the helicopter as she passes, and then turns her head back to the front, stopping abruptly as she comes face to face with something else.

It is a bust, made of sandstone, and it stands on a waist-high pedestal. Although it is the likeness of a man, the features are so rough as to be almost unrecognizable. The sandstone bust has about it a tremendous sense of time, and it is clear that the roughness is caused by erosion.

All the parts of the bust have been carefully labeled, and stenciled letters of dark green paint, spelling FOREHEAD, CHEEK, RIGHT EAR, LEFT EAR, add to the general grotesqueness of the figure. The face, with its disfiguring words, has an expression of such comic sadness that it could never be considered frightening. She tries to rock the statue on its pedestal, but it seems to be firmly bolted into place. She rubs the surface of the bust, and sandstone can be seen crumbling into her hand. Now we see the statue closely it looks very old indeed, as if it has been in this desert for an immense period of time.

She takes out a handkerchief from her handbag, dampens part of it, and tries to rub off part of the "N" in the word "NOSE," and, after considerable effort, the green begins to fade. She runs her fingers over the forehead, and smiles at the "MOUTH" and "CHIN" notices.

She appears to be delighted with the statue.

Slow cello music is now on the sound track.

It is now obvious that the bust is severely eroded.

Although quite clearly signposted, the right and left nipples are no longer distinguishable, and the right armpit is badly chipped. The girl walks behind the statue, and the next shot is from this position, with the girl walking across the frame, round to the front again. From here the bust is even less like a person, and it seems also to lose all its identity as an object, and to fuse into the contours of the desert.

The cello music becomes grotesque and poignant.

From the front again. The girl is peering closely at the statue's face. A dark mark is running across the letters of the "LEFT EYE" notice, making it difficult to read. It can be seen that the mark is in fact moisture, black against the dry stone. She puts out her finger to the dampness, and then touches her tongue to fingertip. The wet area seems to be increasing in size, and the girl begins to look a little apprehensive.

Then she drops her handbag and stares with a profound horror, as a drop of water comes from the left eye and merges with the general wetness. Now an identical darkness is spreading across the other cheek. Another drop comes from the left eye and courses its way down to the chin, leaving a trail that glistens in the sunlight. There is no movement, no sound other than the wide sweeps of the cello melody. The only motion is of the little drops that roll down the figure's rough cheeks.

She steps back appalled. She seems to be incapable of action.

A drop comes from the right eye, and rolls down the craggy face.

She stands with her mouth open, her hands clenching at her sides, staring helplessly at the old, old statue that is now weeping before her. The tears of the statue somehow make real the weight of centuries that have passed in this place. She buries her face in her hands, and looks at the bust no longer.

After about half a minute she takes her hands away.
A certain calmness has spread over her. She slowly picks
up her handbag and feels into it, bringing out a large note-
book. She tears out a page and fashions the paper into a
rectangular shape, then tears one end to a point. She
takes out a fountain pen and writes a single word on the
paper. She fixes the notice to the cheek with a pin, in such
a way that the arrowhead is indicating the water which is
now streaming down the face.

The notice says, simply, "TEARS."

She turns, and swiftly walks away across the desert.

THE FLORISTS

Now the cello has stopped. All that can be heard is the
ironic funeral march from the first symphony of Mahler.
The girl is walking across the desert toward a hill, the only
feature in the otherwise gently sloping terrain, apart
from a black plume of smoke which is rising distantly in the
air. As she gets nearer to this oily cloud of smoke, scurrying
human activity can be seen on the ground beneath.
Occasionally a gout of bright flame bursts along the
ground, and more smoke is added to the cloud, rising swiftly
in the air. Now the camera, in a tracking shot, reveals a
close-up of the girl's face as she walks along. At first lines
of concentration furrow her forehead as she tries to make
out what is going on, then the concentration is replaced
by bewilderment, and then, a little later, by anger. Now the
camera is static, and we see the whole scene as the girl
walks up.

Men in shirt sleeves are rushing about, their faces grimy
and shining with sweat. They look bewildered and panic-
stricken, but this is obviously their normal state of mind.
On their backs they carry the large chemical tanks of
flamethrowers, and the straps have rubbed into their shoulders for so long that they are obviously in great pain. All
around, the ground is seared and black. It appears that

nothing could possibly grow in such a devastated place, but straggly vegetation is visibly thrusting itself up through the soil. Every moment one of the strange plants is beginning to bloom. A bud appears, almost instantaneously, and begins to open. Lush, colored petals are visible, promising future beauty. But as soon as one of the men sees this he moves up and immerses the plant in a bath of flame from the nozzle of the weapon he is carrying. All that is left when the fire dies away is charred black soil. But after only a few seconds, pushing up through this inhospitable earth, can be seen a new plant.

The girl clearly doesn't like this place, but when one of the men comes close to her, a fevered expression on his face, she lightly touches his arm.

GIRL: What is this? What are you doing?

MAN: Killing them.

GIRL: But—why?

MAN: To stop them from growing.

(The man turns away to spread a carpet of flame, and then turns back to the girl.)

The only way is to kill them. If we weren't doing this good work they'd be spreading all over the desert.

GIRL: But why do you want to stop them?

MAN: We don't want these—these filthy blossoms all over the desert. For one thing they'd encourage laxness—all our men would be too lazy to do any useful work, like they're doing now.

GIRL: But the only reason they're working is to kill the flowers.

MAN: And besides which, we're used to the desert. When I see those disgusting petals coming out I feel a strange —tension—inside me. What would happen if I gave way to that, and watched them evolving all the way? And anyway, why are you so interested? I don't like the kind of talk you're giving me.

GIRL: It's just that I can't understand you. You're killing

something that's beautiful and alive, something that can
grow and give you pleasure. . . .
The man looks at the girl with a disgusted expression on
his face, and quite deliberately spits at the ground by her
feet. Then he turns back to his work. But just before
his face goes out of frame his expression can be seen to
change from one of disgust to an infinite sadness. The
music fades.

THE FLAGELLANTS

The girl is now standing on one of the foothills of the
large natural mound in the desert. She stands with her
back to the camera, watching an extraordinary scene taking
place about fifty feet below on the sand. There is a vast
circle of naked people on the plain. Their heads are downcast, and they tramp slowly round, their eyes to the
ground, like prisoners exercising in a large yard. As they
slowly move, each person brings down the lash of a large
whip on to the back of the person before him. This
whipping is so arranged that as one man feels the bite of
the lash on his flesh, his own whip is whistling down,
striking the person in front a fraction of a second later, the
lash of this man about to contact the back of the man
before him. Thus, from a distance, this movement
can be seen to form a wave of energy, which ripples quickly
round the circle, much faster than the people are walking, a wave of pain which circles eternally.

THE EYE

The girl is walking through a complex of corridors,
green walls rapidly moving across the screen. The floors are
of black polished marble, and the sounds of her steps are
echoed by the walls. She turns right, down another
identical corridor, and quickly left again. All the corridors

are the same, and the wooden doors have to distinguish
them only small silver numbers set above them, but the
individual figures cannot be seen. The sounds of her shoes
are now very loud on the sound track, and the echoes build
up in feedback, echoes of echoes, until there is nothing
but a continuous hollow sound, the resonance of the
corridors forming a throbbing note, punctuated by the
clicking of the shoes, which, all the time, are adding still
more sound to the whole.

She suddenly turns and opens one of the doors. We see
her from inside the room as she slams the door shut and
leans against it. The slam of the door terminates the sound
on the optical track, and there is now no noise at all,
nothing but an unnatural silence.

On a table in the middle of the room is a movie
projector. The girl switches off the room light, and goes
across to this table. Light filters into the room through the
drawn venetian blinds, and a large white screen can be
seen dimly at the end of the room. The girl switches on
the projector, and the screen is filled with light. We see,
projected on to the screen, a picture of a girl, walking
hurriedly down a series of green corridors, the floors of
which are of black polished marble. She turns right and
then quickly left again, moving rapidly past many wooden
doors with small silver figures above them. She opens one
of the doors, and can then be seen from inside the room
as she slams the door and leans against it. On a table in the
middle of the room is a movie projector. The girl switches
off the light, and goes across to the projector. A large
white screen can be seen dimly at the end of the room.
She bends down and presses a switch on the side of the
projector.

On the screen is projected the gigantic image of a human
eye. The iris is a light watery blue, and the eye itself,
separated as it is from the rest of the face, expresses nothing
at all. It is just a blue eye, watching all the time.

On the film in the room, the camera begins to approach
the eye, and the silhouetted shape of the girl disappears
on one side of the screen. Now on that film there is nothing
but the blue eye. The girl turns off the projector, and the
picture dies. She turns to face the camera, which tracks
in, closer and closer, until now only her face can be seen,
now only the brow, eye, and cheek, and now just her
staring eye.

THE SWITCHED-ON PSYCHEDELIC AUTO-DESTRUCTIVE CATHEDRAL

The inside of the cathedral batters the eyes and the ears.
Everywhere there is color; the pastel mosaics of the altar,
tapestries, stonework; and bright garish colors, the lights,
the revolving stained-glass windows, the projected beams
staining the clouds of steam. A notice in pseudo-gothic
script, painted in dayglo colors says PSYCHEDELIC FREAK-
OUT—TONITE! In the nave of the cathedral, in front of the
altar, are enormous steam engines. Great pistons, their
brass-work reflecting back the iridescent greens and reds of
the projector, operate powerfully, flashing and gleaming.
Wheels are turning, and great clouds of steam are rising
to the cathedral ceiling, almost invisible due to the sea of
color below. These steam engines drive the windows and the
other moving parts of the cathedral. The windows are
circular, and are of stained glass. They are built in two
layers, each with a bright mosaic pattern. The inner of each
pair of windows is set in a ball-race and revolves slowly, the
colors of both windows combining and separating, forming
new colors, and the patterns of the mosaics working
together, forming moving lines and swirling shapes. A
projector is throwing incandescent colors on to a large
screen set behind the altar, which there form swiftly
alternating patterns of red, green, blue, blinding white,
purple, bright yellow, mauve, orange, in hundreds of
shades. Set all round the cathedral, stroboscopic lights are

flashing, all out of synchronization, and here and there, among the large number of people in the nave, one or two figures are on the floor, writhing in the throes of *grand mal*.

The cathedral is full of sound. Electronic noises are booming through stereophonic loudspeakers set in a ring round the nave, and the sounds chase each other in circles; three cardinals play electric guitars, and a trio of women, their long hair streaming, scream loudly and trace with their hands the shapes of space. The steam engines cannot be heard. A man is standing at the altar with a microphone, brandishing a crucifix. "Turn on!" he shrieks. "Tune in! Drop out!" The robes of the cardinals swirl as their synchronized arms smash down, electronic chords bursting from the loudspeakers.

The girl, her dress now a rainbow-dress, gleaming in the lights of the cathedral, turns and goes through the door. Outside, we see her emerge. Here it is as it was before; there is the desert and the sun, and only faintly can be heard the sounds of the cathedral. She walks hurriedly away. For a long time can be seen nothing but her feet, treading swiftly over the desert sand. When she is a long way from the building, there is a loud crack, and she turns to look. The cathedral appears for a moment to shake, and, abruptly, there is no longer a cathedral, but a vast moving mass, pouring to the ground like a waterfall, surrounded by clouds of dust which obscure the end. On the sound track there is an enormous rumbling crash, and when it has died, and when the dust has settled, there is nothing but a pile of rubble in the desert and a silence that seems infinite. She turns and walks out of frame, leaving, for a moment, the camera trained on the pile of debris, which looks as if it has been there for a million years.

THE CRUCIFIXION

The girl is again walking across the white sand of the desert. The camera pans to follow her as she walks past. On

the sound track is the noise of a strong wind. As she stops
and looks up, into the picture comes the base of a black
marble construction. It is very large and is oval in shape;
only part of it is in the field of view. It consists of oval
slabs, each a little smaller than the one below it, forming an
oval staircase. The marble gleams in sunlight.

Looking down from the top of the edifice. The girl can
be seen climbing the staircase. A black shadow falls
across her, but its outlines cannot be seen clearly. As she
climbs the camera zooms back, so that we see that the
black construction is much larger than it had appeared. As
more and more comes into our field of view, we are able
to see more clearly the shape of the shadow. Abruptly
we see that the shadow is in the form of a cross.

She reaches the top of the construction, walks forward,
and stops. There is blood running down the base of the
cross and forming a small pool beneath it.

From the side. Her face is in frame, at the bottom left.
On the right is the cross, with two bent legs, nailed by
the feet, at the top of the frame.

GIRL: Oh! What have they done to you?

The man on the cross can now be seen entirely. The
upper half of his body is sagging away from the cross, only
the great nails driven through his wrists holding his
weight. Congealed blood lines his arms. His head is hanging
forward, and he regards the girl from under his brows,
with great burning eyes. His flesh is very white, and
his whole body hangs like that of a corpse.

GIRL: Oh! You're in such pain!

MAN (irritably): Of course I'm in pain.

GIRL (almost crying): I must get you down.

MAN: No, you must not. For my name is Jesus Christ of
Nazareth, and it is ordained that I die in this way.

GIRL: But I can't let you suffer like this!

JESUS CHRIST (irritably): My dear girl, this is bad
enough, without you adding to my misery with your

witless comments. If you knew how much this hurt you'd
have more consideration than to make me worry about
anything else. Now leave me alone, and don't attempt
to get me down.

GIRL: Well—do you mind if I talk? Perhaps I will be able
to ease your last hours. And I—I want to talk to you.

JESUS CHRIST: It's immaterial to me; I'll be joining my
Father soon, and I don't give a damn about anything
else.

GIRL: Well, what I need really—I know it's not fair to ask
you at a time like this, but—well—I need help, you see.

JESUS CHRIST: That's my job.

GIRL: You see, I've seen so much today, and—well—I just
wonder about the things I've seen; I suppose I feel a
little confused about it all.

JESUS CHRIST: Don't be confused, my child, for you are
like a lamb, and I am your shepherd. Just follow me,
take the path I show you, and I will lead you to my
heavenly fold.

GIRL: Yes, I appreciate that, but I want to find my own
way around. It can't be wrong, I guess, because you
made me like this. I don't really want to be led anywhere. I've made mistakes, but I've seen a lot of people
today who've made far worse ones than me. I don't
want to contradict, but with all respect, I'm not a
sheep.

JESUS CHRIST: But my child, you are a sheep. For my
Father is in control of the whole universe. He knows
all the secrets of the proton, the quasar, and all the
millions of things of which humans are not even aware.
My Father is all.

GIRL: Well, why am I unhappy?

JESUS CHRIST: Because you have sinned. You are black and
steeped in the foul brew of fleshly wickedness. You
choose the easy path of earthly pleasure, and your soul
drips with evil poison, one drop of which will be enough

to send it screaming to eternal damnation. And you
probably play with yourself.

GIRL: I think you are very rude, and you're not at all as
I imagined you to be. Not only that, you seem very
stupid, for you know nothing about me, what I am, and
yet you criticize me. You seem to me a very shallow
person.

JESUS CHRIST (angrily): What do you mean? If I weren't
nailed up here I'd come down and . . . What do you
mean?

GIRL: I know more about you than you do of me. I know
that you are a man full of compulsive rituals, neurotic,
almost insane. You wouldn't even let me get you down
from the cross because it would upset your precious
ceremonies. They say you are kind, but I don't find
you to be.

JESUS CHRIST (somewhat nervously): Come now, my
child . . .

GIRL (dramatically): You claim omnipotence for your
Father. Well then, in making that claim you are also
claiming for him credit for all the crimes of the universe!
I charge your Father with creating starvation. I charge
him with cruelty, with disease, with disaster. I charge
the God of Love with being the God of Syphilis. I
charge the God of Life with being the God of Death!

JESUS CHRIST: You are on earth, my child, as a test. Only
when you have been weeded, the good from the bad,
can my Father know who to take with him into
eternal life.

GIRL: So, your Father chooses to test us by suffering?
He cannot find another way?

JESUS CHRIST: You cannot understand my Father's
motives, my stupid child. His ways are mysterious to
such as you.

GIRL: But there's no mystery. I am unhappy, and I've
seen people today so unhappy that they didn't even

know it, frightened and lonely people; what have they
done that they should be so punished?
(Dark clouds are banking up very rapidly behind the
    cross. The girl puts one hand on her hip, and points at
    Jesus in a very melodramatic manner.)
So I judge your Father, and I find him guilty. I pronounce
    your Father evil! He knows the universe, you claim,
    the secrets of eternity, yet he cannot understand the
    sadness in a young girl's heart!
    It has become very dark. Jesus Christ suddenly con-
vulses and vomits, fluid pouring down the front of his
body. He begins to twitch on the cross, the muscles knot-
ting and relaxing. His convulsions make him hiccough
violently for a long time. Dark clouds are now filling the
sky, but the girl can still be seen, pointing at the tortured
hanging figure. A flash of lightning suddenly strikes the
cross with an enormous explosion. The cross rips like a
curtain, and in the flash pieces of wood can be seen flying
everywhere. Smoke rises faintly in the air. It darkens
rapidly. Now nothing can be seen but the faint whiteness
of the girl's dress, and the rain which is now falling from
heaven.

THE ENCHANTED FLOWER FIELD

It is sunny, and on the sound track the calls of hundreds of birds can be heard. In front of the camera is a
moving mass of colors. This is the flower field. Gigantic
blossoms are spread in profusion to the horizon. The girl
enters the frame from the side, and stands for a moment
looking at the flowers. Their blossoms are composed of
large fleshy petals, red, white, mauve, purple, orange,
sky-blue, bright yellow, every conceivable color lifted to
the sun in folds of scented flesh. The flower field is like a
thick musky carpet, and the girl takes a deep breath, as if
the air is heady with the perfumes of the flowers. Round

about the bases of these enormous blossoms, green leaves
are intertwined, and large bees are bumbling about from
flower to flower.

The girl steps forward, into the field, an expression of
happy wonderment on her face. She looks at the moment
like a child, but the colors of the flowers have changed
her face into a thing of radiance. The reds and yellows
are reflected in the surface of her skin, and her face is
now the face of a Madonna. At once she is waist-deep in
the flowers. It is as if they strain to meet her. She puts
out her hand and touches the blooms, and they respond to
her touch, the large flat petals stiffening, opening the
cups of their flowers to her hand. She smiles happily, and
begins to sink down among the flowers. The sensual
blooms sway toward her and away, unimaginably beautiful. There is a humming in the air, like the humming
of approaching unconsciousness. The girl disappears into
the midst of the field, and now only the colors of the
swaying flowers can be seen, forming bright shapes all
over the screen.

But a sudden sense of unreality comes over the whole
scene, and then, abruptly, the whole of the flower field
fades away. There is just left the girl, sitting on the sand of
the desert. She looks about herself, terrified and unhappy.
The picture becomes dimmer; this is the end of the film.
But as the picture fades, we notice little green shoots
appearing all over the ground, and we know that it will
not be long before the flower field is back, with all its
radiant glory.

Fade out.

Polite applause.

The Time Machine

THE CELL IS NOT LARGE. There is just room for a small
bunk along one wall, and a small table on the other side,
a stool in front of it. The table and the stool had once
been painted a glossy red, but their finish has long been
spoiled by time, and now light wood shows through the
streaks of paint. The floor is flagged, and the walls are
made of large blocks of stone. The stone has streaks of
dampness across its surface, and in the air is a sweet smell
of decay. There is a window high in the far wall, set
with bars of rusted iron, and through it can be seen a
patch of blue sky, and a wisp of yellow cloud. Sometimes,
not very often, a bird flashes across the space like a brief
hallucination. In the opposite wall there is a large metal
door, with a grill set into its surface. Behind the grill is a
shutter, so that those outside may, when they wish,
observe the prisoner from a safe distance.

The bunk is made of metal, and is fixed permanently to
one wall. It is painted green, and this color is interrupted
only where the rusty nuts and bolts extrude. On one side
the bunk is bolted to the wall, and on the other it is
supported by two metal legs, which have worn little

depressions in the stone floor. Above the bunk, crudely
scratched into the wall are various drawings and messages.
There are initials, dates, obscenities, and phallic drawings. Set a little apart from the others is the only one
which does not make immediate sense. It is engraved
deeply into the wall, and consists of two words, set one
above the other. The engraving obviously took a great deal
of time to complete. The upper of these words is TIME,
the lower, SOLID.

The bunk is covered by rumpled gray blankets, which
smell of the sweat of generations of prisoners. Sitting at
the foot of the bunk is the prisoner. He is leaning over, his
elbows on his knees, his back hunched, looking at a
photograph in his hands.

The photograph is of a girl. It is just a little larger than
two inches square, and is in black and white. It is a
close-up, and the lower part of her arms and her body
below the waist are not revealed. Her head is not directly
facing the camera, and she appears to be looking at something to one side, revealing a three-quarter view of her
face. Behind her is a brick wall—a decorative wall in
Holland Park on that day after the hotel and after the
morning in the coffee shop; soon they were to part again at
the railway station.

Her dark hair was drawn back, and she had a calm but
emotional expression on her face. Her face was fairly
round, but her high cheekbones caused a slight concavity
of her cheeks, giving her always a slightly drawn look
which he had always found immensely attractive, ever
since he had first known her. Her features were somewhat negroid—"a touch of the tar-brush, as my mother
used to put it" she had said in one of her letters—large
dark eyes, and large lips which, when she smiled, gave her
a look of ironic sadness. Occasionally she also had the
practical look of a Northern housewife, and her energy
was expressed in her face and her body. Her body was

very slim, and her flesh felt like the flesh of no other
woman on earth. When he had first seen her she had been
wearing a black dress at a party, a dress which did nothing to conceal the smallness of her breasts, and which
proudly proclaimed her slightness. This had captivated
him immediately. It was something which accented her
femininity, although doubtless she had not considered it in
this way, and he saw her that first time as the most beautiful thing on earth.

He would meet her in Leicester. He would set off early
on Sunday and take a train to Victoria, and walk among
the few people about at this time on a Sunday morning to
the coach station. He could never understand why it
was—as he sat in the cafeteria with a cup of coffee—that
the people all about appeared so ugly. The only people
that morning who were at all pleasing to the eye were
a family of Indians who had sat near him—the women
in saris, and the men bewhiskered and proud in turbans.
Perhaps it was all subjective, and everyone appeared ugly
because he knew that this morning, in little more than
three hours, he would be meeting her again. The weather
was not impossibly cold—they wanted to make love, and
many things were against it that week. At nine-fifteen
he would walk over, past the coaches for Lympne airport
and France, to the far corner of the yard, where the
Leicester coach would be waiting.

He got in the coach. There were never more than eight
or nine people who wanted to go to Leicester early on a
Sunday morning, and he would walk down to the back of
the coach and sit on the left-hand side. Why always the
left he didn't know. At nine thirty-five the vehicle would
set off, pouring out clouds of diesel smoke, emerging from
its home like a mechanical dragon. As they passed Marble
Arch, Swiss Cottage, and headed for the M1, he was
conscious of a mounting tension. Partly sexual—partly
the knowledge that soon he would see her again—and

partly because he knew that *he* knew. What was going to
happen this time? He could visualize that one morning
she wouldn't come, but *he* would, and instead of loving
there would be hatred and fighting. She had told him
during the week, and he had been very upset. But he
wanted her to continue, for he knew what it would do to
her to have to stop now. What had been set into action
was a series of circumstances that had to run a certain
course until it was possible to break it. And the breaking
would be hard—was hard.

The sun was shining, and the fields that they passed
became transformed, as they always did, by her proximity
in time. Everything around him was beautiful. It was as
if he could see the scene through the coach window
with an intensity that would not be possible normally. It
was as if together they were one being, and that apart from
her he was less than half a person. But there were four
other people who depended on her as well. Two little boys,
one little girl, and one adult man. A family is a complete
entity as well. Later he would go to her home in West
Cutford, and see her with her children, and feel himself
to be a malevolent force, a wildly destructive element
that didn't belong here, and yet, seeing at the same time
an image of what might have been; how close was this
reality to the one he wanted.

When the coach left the motorway, it was only half an
hour before he would be in Leicester, and three quarters
before they would be together, their proximity having an
astronomical rightness, as implacably correct as the orbit of
the earth. The watery January sun shone on to the brown
brick buildings that told him that soon he would be at
their meeting-place—the coach station in Southgate
Street. This place had a special significance for him; it
was like the scene of some great historical event. But most
of the places were; not the hotel, where the coming and
going of other people obscured the significance of their

own, but their little shed at Groby Pond, their room at
the top of a house in West London. All these places
deserved some kind of immortality.

Now the tension was very strong; his muscles were
clenched all over his body and his hands were shaking.
The coach approached some traffic lights, turned left,
bumping over a rough road surface, and went down a grim
street, full of half-demolished buildings. Further down
were some other buildings composed of reddish-brown
brick, except for a modern pub which was opposite a large
flat area surrounded by metal railings. The coach turned
into this concrete area, for this was Southgate Street. As
the coach slowed up the few people inside began to rise,
putting on overcoats and collecting their luggage.
He looked intently through the windows to see if she
had arrived. She wasn't here yet. The coach was early; it
was only quarter-past twelve. There was six and a half
hours of the day left. This was always the most difficult
part. Before he had felt that he was going toward her; that
he could feel the distance between them lessening. But
now all the movement was up to her, and he could
no longer be directly aware of it.

He climbed down from the coach and went to the other
side of the road, waiting for her car to arrive. Looking
across at the coach station, he knew that he would remember this place for the rest of his life, whatever happened.
In one month, seventeen days and six hours they would
say goodbye for the last time.

Cars were passing in groups; there would be a time
when nothing was on the road at all, then later twenty cars
would come along together, and his eyes would move as
he looked at first one, then the next. A cold wind was
blowing, and he was shivering uncontrollably. A couple of
girls walked past on the other side of the street, talking
and laughing together. A car came along that looked like
hers, but inside it was a large, white-haired man. This

was impossible. He turned and walked round to the
entrance of the pub. This was "The Shakespeare," the
same name as another pub that had featured in their
lives; it was as if their whole existence was marked out by
commonplace things that were all cryptograms, that all
had hidden significance. Their love made everything more
real, and at the same time turned the world into a devious
collection of symbols.

He pushed through the doors of the pub, and went
into the lounge bar. He ordered a drink, and then went
to sit by one of the windows. If he stood up and looked
through the net curtains he could just see part of the coach
station. Parked outside was a car, but from here it did
not look like hers. He sat down, and regarded the shiny
surface of the table in front of him.

Things were obviously bad for her at home. Her letters
had told him what had been going on. She could not
get away from this situation; she would part from him
and then go back to a person who was being hurt, a person
whose life was being threatened by their love—a love that
seemed innocent and inevitable. That first night, when
they had suddenly found themselves in bed together, when
a few hours before they had been little more than friendly
strangers, it had all seemed so right. They both knew that
life was now going to become difficult, but still wanted
it to happen. He stood up, and peered through the window.
The parked car was still there, and she was not in sight.
He sat down again. But how much stress could one stand?
How much could this man stand? He understood the
situation, but how long would it be before his control
broke down, and he came with nothing in his brain but
an urge to destroy? How would he react to this? How
could he possibly try to physically hurt a man he had
hurt so much already? He stood up and looked through
the window again. Suddenly finding it impossible to wait
in the pub any longer, he abruptly walked toward the

door and went outside in the cold again. The parked car
was not hers. It was nearly half-past twelve. He crossed
the road and went back inside the coach station. He sat
down on a bench with his back to the road. In his bag
was a book, and he took it out. It was very cold. He began
to read.

The sun has passed the point at which it shines directly
into the cell. Now dark shadows are creeping across the
floor, and it is becoming colder. The prisoner lifts his
feet from the floor and lies back on his bunk, holding the
photograph above him. At the time the photograph had
been taken they had spent two days in a room in a hotel
in London, doing little but making love, going out
occasionally for food. It had been a fairly cheap hotel, and
the room had looked, at first, rather bare. But in two
hours it had become transformed into a jeweled palace.
The red bedcover had glowed with the mystical luminosity
of a robe in a Flemish painting. When they had left the
hotel, they had gone to Holland Park, aching to make
love again, full of an insatiable desire to repeat an
experience so good it should have been unrepeatable. He
felt vaguely surprised that the exposed flesh of her face
and neck did not show any signs of his love. He felt that
his hands and lips and tongue should have left visible
tracks on her skin that would show that this woman was
loved. Perhaps there was a gentleness in her eyes, a quirk
of her lips, but perhaps he was imagining these signs.

He held the photograph close to his eyes so that he
could see the grain, and the slight fuzziness of her
individual hairs. Now he was conscious of the photograph
as a record only. A piece of paper that was not even there
at the time. Recorded tracks of light that had reflected
from her at that time into the lens of a camera. This
contact with her was so nebulous, and yet the photograph
somehow solidified the events, gave them a concrete
reality, as if at some time or some place they were together

in Holland Park, she in front of him, apologizing for her tiredness and the untidiness of her hair, saying "Just after making love is not the best time for taking a picture of me," and then being quiet and looking to one side, and the shutter opening, slowly, slower, and then freezing, wide open, this "time" a tangible material like film going through a camera, that can be wound on, stopped and taken out.

Their love affair was now like a piece of sculpture, an object that plainly begins at one point and ends at another, but which may be seen as a single object in space, which may be looked at closely, details expanding, may be examined from different angles, touched, embraced, wept upon.

The last time in the hotel had been good, so good that he could now remember nothing but an ecstatic feeling of life and death and her cries regularly punctuating the quiet of the room, and his own gasped sounds joining hers in a complex of rhythm, and then nothing but his own engulfment in a torrent of whiteness.

Caroline Howard. First just a name, and then a name that was a woman, and then a name that was so intertwined with his own existence it became a million things, was a part of him. Just the sound of her name, reflected softly from the stone walls was enough to bring back a whole series of memories and associations; it must be like the lifetime's memories of a drowning man. In a fraction of a second it was all there to be seen, touched, tasted, smelled. Caroline Howard Caroline Howard Caroline Howard—a bright orgasm in morning sunlight.

The time machine operates on an organic, electrochemical basis, with mineral connections. It is operated by means of a circulating substance that is sometimes fluid and sometimes gaseous, passing through an infinite number of stages of creation. This substance becomes

finer and finer in form, eventually phasing from the limits
of existence to great solidity and density, beginning the
cycle again. The implications of this cycle, with the
relative nature of its stages, provide the basic crystallizing
power of the machine. The apparatus is also provided
with gross mechanical parts, cogs, motors, and chains,
which are essential to the smooth transport of its medium
through all the stages of metamorphosis. The machine
deals with relationships, patterns, and similarities. Some
of the implications of the time machine are almost
metaphysical in nature.

It may easily be seen that the machine is not like any
other of the mechanical constructions that have been
made up to now. While the operation of the machine may
be analyzed in detail, the reader of such a description will
not be able to understand the functions of its cycles. Also
the mechanically-minded reader will notice immediately
that there are components which he would deem unnecessary and uneconomic, and he will undoubtedly comment,
too, that more components seem to be essential for the
machine to be able to operate, and that in its present
state it would be capable of doing absolutely nothing.
The time machine is in fact capable of operation in a
number of different ways. It may work on a human
being, who may attach himself to the machine, which
will then, by means of juxtaposition of the medium with
parts of his body, function on him in a completely physical way. On the other hand it may work in a more
general sense for one, or any number of separate observers.
Also, the machine may, and does, operate entirely on its
own, unobserved; it does this constantly, the separate
parts of the construction existing at different and all
points of time.

It is to be understood that time is not a moving stream.
Time is a minor quality of the continuum, common
only to living creatures, and consists of an involuntary

change of attention. The consciousness of a creature is an infinitely restricted series of sense-impressions, operating in three dimensions only. The universe consists of a four-dimensional geometric form, which, in cross section, contains all the physical facts of matter, and is curved so that it eventually rejoins itself, forming a four-dimensional ring shape. Thus, a cross section of any part of this ring, will produce the universe at any particular point in "time." This "time" is merely the attention of the creature observing the shape about him, and is due to his being able to be aware of only one infinitesimal part of the shape. His attention is constantly and involuntarily operating on a different part of the ring, giving the impression of movement and animation to what is in fact a static object, and also giving him the false impression of temporal duration. If one draws a wavy line, and follows this line with one's eyes, it will appear to move up and down, whereas with a widening of attention the line can be immediately appreciated as an unmoving and complete object. The time that each of us experiences is common only to us, and is an internal psychic operation rather than a measurable physical fact.

If we stand at one end of a room and walk across to the other, this restricted attention is all that gives the impression of movement. Movement is in fact an aspect of time, and to someone lacking this restriction of attention, it would be obvious that the movement was only an impression in the mind of the person concerned and that his body, as it crossed the room, was merely a solid and static object.

We can see now that time is not the barrier it was once thought to be, and that as a psychic mechanism it may be radically altered, and completely destroyed. It is surprising that this was not realized before; the time-dilation or time-destruction observed by takers of the "mind-expanding" hallucinogenic drugs has been often

noted, as well as the more usual distortions of time
during various mental states, common to everybody.

The time machine, by operating in terms of relationships of pattern, is able to crystallize the attention of the
observer, producing a concrete *déjà vu*, and in the
solidity of its wheels and pistons, we find reflected the
tangibility of the universe, in all its states of being.

He looked up from the book. And saw her. She was
talking to two bus men, asking them if they knew whether
the London bus had arrived yet. He hurriedly put the
book away, and as he stood she saw him. She was wearing
her black fur coat, and her face, as she came toward him
was his own face, as familiar as the face he shaved each
morning, a face that was more than the sum of all the
faces he knew; his own, his parents', his friends', more
than anything else he would ever find. Her face was
troubled. They approached each other slowly, not running
with joyful exuberance as they had the last time they
had met here, or moving quickly with desperation to clasp
each other, to shut off the world in the closeness of each
other's arms as they would later. He took her gently in his
arms, and they kissed softly, and then embraced, holding
each other tightly. She exhaled his name in a sigh, a
drooping inflection that suggested pressure that had been
building up suddenly released. Now was right; everything
was infinitely right. His face was pressed against her neck,
the scent of her hair was filling his nostrils, her body was
warm in his arms. Now he was alive, and he did not want
to move from this position ever again. His hands ran over
her back, and he felt her lips at his neck; he was melting
into a state of complete being, a state that had intolerable
tensions and unformulated desires, that caused his
breath to be exhaled explosively, hearing the sounds he
made, they both made, to be like miniature versions of
the sounds crushed from their bodies by the dazzling

pressure of orgasm. Waves of pressure ran round his body; his head moved, lips brushing her cheek, her ear, her neck. Their heads drew apart, and he looked into her eyes. He felt his head moving with the impossible surging of communication of emotions impossible to communicate. His eyes moved as he tried to take in all the details of her face at once. He smiled, and saw an answering smile on her face, a reflection of his own bursting feelings. They kissed for a long time, and then slowly drew apart.

"How have things been at home?"

"Not too good. Difficult."

They began to walk out of the coach station, their arms round each other.

"Do you mind if we go for a drink first? I do feel that I need it."

"Of course not."

They walk across the road, and into "The Shakespeare." They sit at the table with drinks, and she opens her coat to reveal her gray dress. He tells her that he is very fond of the dress, and they tell each other "I love you," a universal reassurance, always needed. Soft lips against his. Unhappiness in her eyes. In memory, not much is said. A letter is discussed, and one or two sentences are actually verbalized, although in a constantly varying way. "He can accept the whole thing intellectually, and he doesn't want to stop it, for my sake. He knows I'm seeing you."

"I know."

"No, I mean today. He saw me off, and watched me drive away in the car." A feeling of mute horror that stays the same, despite the changing pattern of the words. "What with my period and everything, all my energies are at a low ebb. I'm in the most schizophrenic state. There's part of me that can't bear the thought of having an affair, and the rest of me wants nothing but you." He says

nothing. There is nothing but the sound of her voice, and
he watches her lips moving, sees the flecks of mascara
on her cheeks, feels terror at his innocent power of
inflicting pain.

Later they leave the pub, at one o'clock, and drive off
to Groby Pond, the place at which they arrived the last
time, his first trip to Leicester, after driving off twelve
miles in the wrong direction, laughing at the confusion
into which they were both plunged by their mutual
proximity. They take a wrong turning this time, and the
next time. At Groby Pond was a disused quarry where they
had come before, to be alone under an enormous sky, a
sky that made no judgments, condemned no one, and
was content to be.

The city is devoted to the appreciation of beauty—
Rolling architecture is spread out in autumn sunlight—
The city has patterned trees set out among the plazas—
High towers pillars for the sky—Spotlights are situated
along the curbs to show the human bodies on the
pavements to their best advantage—Last year a man was
found wearing clothes and was executed—Soft winds blow
scents of musk into the markets—In the main square is
a gigantic golden representation of a single testicle—The
sounds of the people are the muted voice of summer
holidaymakers—laughter on a tennis court—Parks are
rolling grassland with bowers supplied for making love,
which must be made aesthetically—The main crime is
committing offences against the soul, for which the
penalty is instant, and beautiful, decapitation—Birds
shriek into the sun, protesting at the loss of their virgin
cruelty—Sleek, fat cats assume poses in the gutters—Men
urinate only from the tops of high buildings—The
government headquarters consists of five red towers,
standing up in the city like the fingers of a bloody hand—
All the pubs have yards where one may sit with one's

love and drink together for the last time—the courtyards
are like seas—there are no lavatories—illness is forbidden
by state decree—Sculptures are designed to be orgasms
in steel—In a park in the center of the city is a large brick
shed with a light on its side—Serious musicians play
only some Mozart and some Berg—Beaches and pavilions
glisten like mirrors in the sun—The city beats like a bird's
wing—People float in aerial choreography, like the
sinking drowned—Metal is woven in great garlands and
shines throughout the city—Capsules of mescalin are set
in trays at every point—The city is the city of time—the
city knows no time—the city is the city of the soft
people—the city of flags and paintings that move—the
city is the city of the afternoon—mown grass falls from the
sky like rain—The city is the city of beautiful decay,
where all is young—the city is the city of the sky—the
city of eternal surprise—the city of long dark hair—
the city of eggs with marble shells—the city is a diffraction
grating, and from a height of three hundred feet can be
seen only as a blaze of color—It is the city of high
parabolas—the city of impossible waterfalls—the city
of melting silver blades—the city is the city of brooks—
they weave their way everywhere—all the time is the sound
of bubbling water. . . .

The time machine utilizes certain objects for its various
operations: a skull cap with electrodes, attached to a
machine designed for the artificial production of sexual
orgasm; the miniature score of Messiaen's *Chronochromie*;
a magnetic tape, two thousand, four hundred feet long,
containing nothing but the voice of a man repeating the
word "time"; a reproduction of Dali's landscape,
Persistence of Memory; a bracket clock by Joseph Knibb.

He enters the time machine, giving himself up to its
embrace, feeling his normal consciousness changing, the
widening of his perceptions. Colors flow over his body

like a smooth sheet of water—blue sparks ignite in his
brain—he is conscious of the pattern his body makes in
space-time—He moves his finger and sees the resultant
wiggling shape, his finger like an electroencephalograph
pen—Words float in his mind, picked out in violet fire—
Long steel fingers fiddle about in his brain like the legs of
robot spiders—He falls asleep and wakes up three hundred times a second—His feet are removed by steel hands
and placed neatly under his bed—His arms are broken
off with mechanical deftness—his body is taken completely
apart by the mechanical fingers, and he slides in pieces
through the conveyor belts of the machine.

They pulled up at the pond, with the front of the car
only a few yards from the water's edge. There were several
other cars parked here too; this was a fairly popular
beauty spot. A few people were outside their cars, braving
the January weather, throwing pieces of bread to the
ducks on the water. They sat for a while, he with his arm
around her, his face pressed to her hair, stroking her with
slow fingers, their voices low as they spoke to each other,
both of them weighed down by circumstances so vast that
they could not be seen all at one time. She had brought
along a bottle of wine, cheap red wine with brandy added,
a box of sandwiches, and also a thermos flask of coffee.
They filled the cup of the flask with wine, and took turns
sipping from it. "You realize that these are only delaying
tactics on my part? I feel so low. If I really wanted to
make love, I wouldn't want food or anything." He nodded,
for he knew. It was up to her to make the move today.
She offered him a small sandwich, but at the moment he
was unable to eat; his stomach was locked with tension.
But he watched her eating, looking at her as if looking
could lock her forever within him, knowing that in time
the outlines of her features would fade, until one day,
alone, he would remember only a composite picture of her

face, not looking as she looked on this day or at any time.
But still he looked at her intensely, watching the movements of her hands, her glances, and her dark eyes.

They packed away the food, and she came into his arms
again. "In a minute we can go and make love."

"Do you want a cigarette first?" She took a cigarette,
and they stayed smoking for a moment, now and then
drinking from the cup.

Now was the time to leave the car, and they went round
to the trunk, where she had stored an enormous bundle
of blankets, wrapped in a gray oilcloth. She had smuggled
these blankets out of the house so that they should at
least be comfortable. As he helped her with the bundle,
he was very conscious of the people about, as if they knew
that it was full of blankets. Last time they had climbed
over a wide green gate that led to the quarry, but now
they could see a car parked by the gate, full of people
looking out at the sheet of silver that was Groby Pond.
This time, they decided, they should go over a stile a little
further down, set into a low stone wall. They walked
along, he with one arm clasping the bundle, the other
round her, his fingers buried in the fur of her collar. The
last time they had been here they had gone over the green
gate, ignored a small path leading to the left toward a
brick shed and some other buildings in a little dip, and
had taken the right-hand path up to the top of the quarry,
and had lain in the brambles in this incredibly open
place, in which it seemed that there was nothing but a
huge sky and great vistas of gray stone cliffs. Later they
would go through the gate and would turn left, down the
small path, and they would never go over this stile again.
He pushed the blankets under the bottom rung and
climbed over, helping her as she followed. There was a
tortuous path leading downward through the trees and
undergrowth, in the direction of a brook. They began to go
down the path, he leading the way and holding on to her

hand, sliding, being whipped by branches and circum-
navigating patches of mud. Laughing, they came to a little
river of mud, and clambered across it. Now the way
ahead looked even more impenetrable, and even less
likely to lead up to the top of the quarry. He suggested
that she wait here, while he went on to see what was
ahead.

His perspective changes—He rushes along corridors of
people, the same people, in quanta of time, each one
slightly different from the last, like a movie film—A mad
express, lights reflecting from the walls of life.
The time machine poses problems.
Why? Why did they take this path, that second time,
when later they would find a much easier way to get to
their little shed? Why did they not brave the stares of the
people in the car, and avoid this tortuous journey? Why,
the first time, did they go over the green gate but completely ignore the path that led to their refuge? The shed at
Groby Pond was so important to them. They even called
it their "den." It was a little enclosed world of three sides,
in which they could shut out the knowledge of pain and
the niceties of balance that were necessary for them to stay
whole. They could observe this world outside through a
missing fourth wall, only partly masked by stringy bushes,
and could hear its water bubbling nearby. Why did they,
then, choose not to go down the small path on these two
occasions? It is not only in love, but in all life that people
often act with the blind illogicality of the insane. What
is this quality called "time" that makes them act so?
How can one assess an adulterous love affair seen now in
terms of shape?

He emerged into a clearing. There were some brick
buildings to the right, a couple of sheds, and a cottage
with boarded-up windows. He went over to try the doors

but found them locked. He found that he was concen-
trating on this moment of being alone, living it with a
perverse kind of enjoyment, like the enjoyment of being
cold just before stepping into a warm bath. He turned.
Behind him was a shed with three sides. It was about five
feet high and very roomy. The front was half-concealed
by straggly bushes, and the darkness inside should hide
the glimmer of two bodies, unless someone got too close.
He walked across to the shed, and went inside. He was
rather disappointed by the interior, which was gloomy
and damp. He came out of the shed again, wondering
whether or not it would be suitable. He decided to use the
opportunity of this solitude to urinate, smiling as he
unzipped his fly, at this unexpected modesty of his, and
feeling rather ashamed of it at the same time. Hearing
her coming, he forced the process even faster and barely
finished before she appeared from behind the buildings.
Feeling a little like a guilty schoolboy, he zipped up his
trousers and went toward her. "I've found a place," he
said, "but you may find it a bit sordid." She walked across
to the shed and looked inside. "Why, it's perfect. But
will we be seen from the road?" He stepped back until he
was a long way away. He could see her now as only a
vague patch of lightness in the shed. "No," he called,
"it's fine!" He came back, and picking up the bundle of
blankets he carried them inside the shed. He put the
bundle down, and then took her in his arms. They kissed,
their bodies pressed together, and his general tension was
suddenly transformed into sexual desire, his body
responding to hers with a swiftness that spoke of their
long parting. They drew apart, and she squatted on the
floor and began to unroll the bundle. Inside were two
large blankets, and he was amused to see that she had
even had the foresight to bring a red towel with her.
They spread out the groundsheet, and arranged the
blankets into an improvised double bed. He took off his

sweater and arranged it to serve as a pillow. Now when
they spoke their voices were hushed, and quietly they both
took off their shoes, lifted the blankets, and slid side by
side into their bed in the shed at Groby Pond, while
outside the brook bubbled past.

The time machine caresses with soft winds—it deafens
the mind with brave light—slow blind worms stretch
their bodies through time—straight files of fingers tap on
miles of desks—gray vines are shrined in fog and kick and
scream like young horses—wings are torn from my *back*!

> Gas springs from eight star-formed arms
> Which revolve like pink wheels
> "Ghost" gas is leaked off into the spandrels
> Pressuring a container which explodes
> Pulling a chain which pulls a claw
> Which plucks the tine of a tuning fork
> Sounding a clear A
> Which reorganizes the constituents of the gas
> Stars wheels and spandrels
> Form a double hexagon of mystical significance
> And the gas throbs with the deep blue glow
> Of an unnatural agency
> The shapes of the spandrels—
> Cherubs' faces with foliage—
> Reform the organization of the gas
> Which rings and metamorphoses
> Into lead

The time machine taps his body with a thousand
fingers which play over his skin like a row of pianists. The
fingers have little needles in the tips, which are feeding
a special electrically conductive ink. This ink is tattooed
into his body in a complex pattern, and soon the whirls
and curlicues will flow with an electrical force. Time drips
from a faucet like dark green treacle.

Later they were going to lie together naked in this shed, but this time the coldness and the likelihood of detection made them agree beforehand to keep on as many clothes as possible. Their bodies twisted together, her hands running over him, he kissing her ear, her neck, her throat. They whimper together with the delight of this long-delayed contact. He slides his leg between hers, pressing it high, and feels the muscles of her thighs clenching in response. He unzips her dress, and lowers his face to the flesh of her shoulders and back, this feeling of her flesh against his coming as an actual physical relief, as if, for the rest of his life, when not with her he would always miss the feel of her body. He slid the dress down, exposing the soft dark skin of her chest and arms, and the little brassiere. His mouth found the sweetness of her shoulders, and his lips lingered there. Her hands were on his thighs, and then his shirt was unbuttoned, and her lips were against his stomach. He helped her hands with his belt and trousers, sliding his clothes from his legs completely, and shuddering under the ecstatic pressure of her hands. He felt that their lovemaking could never become banal; each time they came together it was a mutual exploration of pleasure. Each possible contact of their bodies could be repeated a million times. Her dress was now round her neck, and his hands ran over the smooth warm flesh. This time of lovemaking was all times of lovemaking, the little soft mounds of her breasts, her arching stomach, always receiving the caresses of his hands and mouth, never any other. The afternoon was the afternoon of her body; there was nothing else in time or space, nothing but her limbs and her flesh, nothing but the pressure of her hands on his skin. They kissed as if their mouths were drawn together magnetically, until their faces were covered with saliva, and there was nothing but a wide wet world of voluptuous love. Their arms around each other, their bodies surged together at the hips. He slid

her pants down over her legs, caressing the smooth skin
of her limbs, until the scrap of silk disappeared into the
blankets. And now their bodies pressed together with
nothing between them, the feel of their naked flesh making
their kisses even more urgent. His hand circled, running
over her skin, her belly, her thighs, running through a
nest of hair between her legs, circling smaller until it
found puckered flesh, moving up and down slowly, pressing deeper, until his finger finally entered a soft dark
electrical place, and she gasped, and arched her body still
more. He was vaguely expecting to find a string in the
way, but he could feel none, and then forgot about it.
This was Caroline; now she could understand, and so
could he. Time passed, and none was comprehended.
Nothing mattered but the feel of her body. He slid two
fingers inside her, and she caught her breath. His tongue
ran over her stomach, and he rotated his wrist, his fingers
moving in a soft wet place, curves of muscle pressing
them. Her hands were on him, driving everything from
his mind but the consciousness of her and of this exquisite
pressure. He felt a different quality in the wetness of her
vagina, and a long time later realized that there was a
profuse flow of blood. When he finally withdrew his hand,
he slowly moved it up, arching his wrist so that his fingers
did not touch the bedclothes, and brought his hand to
the light. His first two fingers were covered from top to
bottom in thick, bright red blood. She was watching his
hand too; it had suddenly assumed a position of para-
mount importance, like an object framed by perspective
lines in a photograph. What had been an unobtrusive
movement had become a dramatic gesture. He felt as
though he had just been probing a terrible wound in her
body, and had a brief moment of horror. "Have you got
a piece of rag?" She indicated a packet of sanitary pads
that he hadn't noticed before, and he took one, and
quickly wiped the blood from his fingers. She felt his

erection beginning to subside, and asked "Are you sure you want to make love?" He nodded, not thinking of asking her the same question, thinking of nothing but loving her. His hands ran over her again, and soon his body found itself moving over her, now above her, now sliding into the dampness of her.

Now there was a pause.

Now they were together.

He looked down at her face, and kissed her slowly on the lips, running his hands in little repetitive caresses over her bare shoulders. Slow movements began, like the movements of glaciers, years of time translated into flashes of fire. Then faster, now a rhythm. A single strand of bright steel, a long rod that flashed brightly, twirling in the bright electrical air, wider and wider, filling the world with silver. And then he paused, looking down at her face, raising his eyebrows slightly. She smiled. "We haven't seen each other often enough, have we?" He began to move again, feeling the focus of their bodies damply sliding together, the warmth of her flesh next to his. The world revolved about him. He lifted his head, feeling the movement like a ritual of intense importance. And thin strands of wire string out, joining together, forming thicker strands, ropes of wire, less and less, until there is only one rod, gleaming brightly, shining and glittering, twisting and coruscating, growing wider and wider. . . . He stopped his movements again, and then started, slowly. Moving in her he could feel his skin all over his body, his limbs warm, and a nostalgic, dropping emptiness in his stomach. He concentrated on these feelings, trying to blot out the other feeling from his mind —the feeling of sharpness, a diffused sweet whiteness that was even now making itself more manifest, becoming more and more powerful, almost overwhelming. He stopped again, suddenly. He kissed her gently on the lips and spoke. "It's obviously going to be like this all the time.

Will you mind us pausing like this?" "No, no, that's all right." They kissed again, their tongues trembling together, damp surfaces all over their bodies in contact. And he felt his body moving again.

The city is the city of broken festivals—city of changing carpets and the August moon—spires dance in the squares —in the city the night is velvet—instead of drains, set along the gutters are bowls of wild flowers—cats sing among headstones—drunken women in bright flared skirts dance among piles of petals—the city is full of soft waters that fall slowly from the moon—in the center of the city is a tall steel rod that grows wider and wider, opening out at the top into an enormous white umbrella—colored banners are set from building to building, covering the city in bursts of flame—skeletons dance in the city's lights—the festival is a jubilee of eternity—vendors of violet shadows move in a concourse through the streets— crowds of people move like slow pink phantoms—long white worms coil about the lamp standards—the city revolves in the fire of night—stainless steel fingers spread to receive the dawn—festivities ring out among the spider struts—all the people are spread with daffodils. . . .

Their bodies lay together. They were now one being, neither male nor female, but just a complete body of a strange, lethargic creature that twitched, regularly contracting itself under some blankets. He moved in her, feeling her soft moisture, feeling the folds of voluptuous muscle holding him. When they stopped again, they lay over to one side. Now he could caress her, and his hand moved over her back, along her thighs, feeling acres of flesh, fields that he could explore at leisure, feeling too the damp blows at his hips, the feeling of the underside of her body against his abdomen, his testicles rolling back and forth and bumping her. His hand probed beneath her,

feeling the wetness that had run from her, and the
pucker of her anus, trying to ingest the whole of her body,
his stomach sinking and his body melting into hers,
pausing, moving again. Once he had to stop suddenly, and
all his muscles became rigid with the effort of shutting
off, his arms shaking, feeling a spurt of semen, and then
the feelings receding, and now moving vigorously, knowing that they would not return for a long time, looking
down at her face, her swollen lips, her mouth half-open,
her breath exhaled in little sighs, each movement of his
body echoed by hers, a shuddering over the whole of her.

The city shimmers like glass—waltzes fade in dark
alcoves—the sun shatters and falls to the sea like tumbling
drops of blood—wire springs nod in the morning air—grass
dies in profuse movements—fountains are spurting, their
water viscous in death—skulls rattle on pavements—the
city is brown, and the stones crack—flowers are growing
from genitals—the pavements are littered with dying
blooms—the air is sweet with the death of flowers—dye
drips from the banners, bleaching them a pure white. . . .

A sound of water, dim light, and leaves and stones on
the ground. It was as if he was seeing everything with a
preternatural clarity, watching the stones to keep his mind
away from the mass of physical sensations in which he was
floating. Their bodies writhed together on the ground, and
he felt that this movement, this strange dance, had been
going on for eternity, that there had never been any other
life, that he had been born in this woman and would die in
her embrace. His body was floating, he was conscious of
vast chemical reactions going on in the universe. Her breath
was coming in loud gasps now, and he knew that it
wouldn't be long. But he may have to stop, and it may
escape again. A white wedge inserted itself, growing more
and more prominent, and his body began to erupt in a

THE TIME MACHINE   115

silver anguish. He stopped. He was breathless and covered
with sweat. Lying still in her he looked at her face. She
was breathing heavily, and as he watched her face changed,
moving from side to side, all the marks of normal human
life dropping away, her head going back, her mouth open.
Her cries began, slow regular cries, and he began to
move again, letting the feelings blossom, opening the
floodgates, dropping, dropping, a silver line blooming inside
him, higher, higher, but not quite high enough and then
breaking, their movements frenzied, resignation, dimly
hearing his own voice, feeling his head dropping, and then
only a world of whiteness.

The city implodes, the towers, spires and struts of metal
raining to the center like a waterfall—liquid pours in on the
dead city—whirlpools of vegetation—dead people dance
in the water—all that is left is a floating mass of flowers
and machines.

They lay together quietly, and he kissed her, feeling his
body warm and relaxed, with no tension in him anywhere.
She opened her eyes, looking worried. "I wanted to give
you something you could remember, like that time in the
hotel . . ." "It's all right; nothing went wrong. It was
good for me." She smiled at him. "That sometimes
happens. It just starts when I am relaxed." They lay
together some more, and smoked a cigarette. He slowly
withdrew from her, and she handed him the towel as he
kneeled upright. He rubbed the towel over the front
of his body, suddenly realizing that it was pitch dark.
He could feel clots of blood on his flesh, and rubbed
energetically. He lit a match to see how much blood there
was on him. There were a few stains left, and he
wiped at them. In the dim light of the match he could
see the pallid skin of his body, and looking at his
half-erect penis he suddenly felt a revulsion for his

own flesh, and shook out the match. There was congealed
blood all over his hairs, feeling uncomfortable, but he
realized that it would have to stay there until he had time
to wash. They began to search for their clothes by match-
light. "We said we were going to keep on our clothes, but I
managed to lose all mine except my dress, and that was
round my neck!" They laughed together as they searched.
While they were dressing they were quiet, and he wondered
if she too felt this strange melancholy that had settled
on him. He lit another match, and looked at his watch. "It's
half-past five; we were quite a long time. It gives us just
long enough to sit in the car for a while and then get back
to Leicester." They gathered together their possessions,
rebundled the blankets, and emerged from the little shed,
walking slowly past the line of buildings, holding hands, up
toward the road.

They moved carefully through the blackness, seeing
nothing but the dark shapes of trees against the dim sky.
A car briefly flooded the road above with light. As they got
to the higher ground there was a large black shed, with a
single light on the side. The ground was yellow in this light,
which shone on to the surrounding trees, making them
look like pale ghosts. They stood together watching this
light, conscious of the smallness of their bodies and feeling a
strong and inexplicable sadness. The light made everything
cold and unreal, an analytical light that transformed familiar
trees into symbols of unconsummated love and inevitable
death. Her hand tightened round his, and they stood watching the light for a long time. He knew that one day he
would find the events of this day quite amusing, but at the
moment he felt only a sadness fed by the yellow light. They
turned, and walked quickly to the green gate, climbing
over hurriedly. The lake was dark as they walked past, and
all was quiet but for the sound of water lapping at the
shore. There was a car parked near hers, and as they passed
they saw a couple kissing. "Let's tell them that we know a

much better place!" she said, and he laughed as he helped
her squeeze the bundle into the trunk.

They could both keenly feel the cold, and he shivered
as she got in the car and unlocked his door. Inside the car
she switched on the light, and then got out the box of sandwiches. Now he felt hungry, and he ate quickly. There
was congealed blood round his fingernails, but he didn't
want to clean it off, wanting to carry her substances as long
as he could. They sat and talked lethargically, kissing each
other gently. In each other's eyes they could read the urgent
question: "What are we to *do?*" Now there was very little
of the day left. At quarter to six, one hour before they
were due to part again, the car backed out and turned on to
the road, leaving Groby Pond behind it.

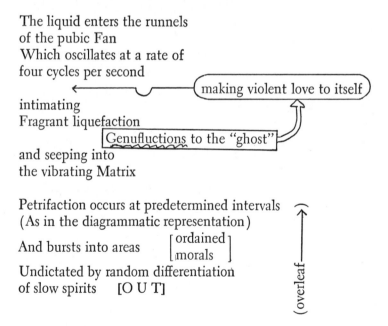

The liquid enters the runnels
of the pubic Fan
Which oscillates at a rate of
four cycles per second

making violent love to itself

intimating
Fragrant liquefaction

Genufluctions to the "ghost"

and seeping into
the vibrating Matrix

Petrifaction occurs at predetermined intervals
(As in the diagrammatic representation)

And bursts into areas   ⌈ ordained ⌉
                        ⌊ morals   ⌋

Undictated by random differentiation
of slow spirits   [O U T]

(overleaf)

The car drew up outside the coach station. The London
coach, a bright looming monster, was ready to leave, and

would shortly be drawing out of the station on its way to the M1. As the car pulled up outside "The Shakespeare" they turned and fell into each other's arms. Her lips were frantic on his, and they pressed tightly to each other, wanting to make love again, wanting to hold the other and never let go. Soon, very soon, they would leave, and the distance between them would expand rapidly, at a combined rate of one hundred and twenty miles per hour. His right hand was under her coat, running over her shoulder and back, trying to impress the feel of her on his mind for ever. She pulls the front of her sweater out of her skirt and thrusts his cold hand up against the warmth of her body. They meet for polite conversation in a pub. She sits over an armchair, her legs dangling over one arm, listening to Messiaen's *Trois Petites Liturgies*. They talk together in the yard of Henekey's in Portobello Road on a bright sunny day, thinking that time was more crucial to them then than ever before, their words measured now only in hundreds. Cogs turn, and the time machine performs a ritual osculation at the foot of a metal apparition. The city swirls in autumn tides, its drowned coiling like ropes, the bodies illuminated by the sunny greenness of the water, hair forming moving curves, skin shredding off in twisting rinds, fixed by the sun above in a moment of coiling, gentle—beauty. They meet again, hurriedly taking off their clothes and making love on a living room carpet. They die. They are born. The birds of night flap through years, their large black wings dripping yellow drops of poison. The universe rolls through the ether like a dead whale. They kiss, trying to merge into each other, tongues searching for this union which will bind them forever. The car door opens. He leaps out and walks quickly across to the coach. He sits by a window, and a girl sits beside him. As the coach moves off he watches her car, and sees her sitting inside in the darkness, watching the coach.

They do not wave to each other.

The prisoner feels in the right-hand pocket of his denim suit. He pulls out a small leather wallet, and puts the photograph into one of the compartments, transferring it back to the pocket. Now it is evening; the stone walls are touched with gold. He lies on his back on the bunk, watching the ceiling, and the rippling spider webs. A little while later there is a rattling sound at the door. Soon it opens, and his warder walks in. He turns his head on the bunk and looks at the warder.

The man clears his throat and then begins to speak, as if speaking is an effort.

"There has been a general decree. All the prisoners are to be released. You are free to go."

PHILIPS' "FORGOTTEN MASTERS" SERIES

Symphony No. 6 in C minor
THE TRAGIC
by Ludwig van Beethoven II

PERHAPS IF A POLL were to be taken of professional musicians, less than one percent would admit to having heard of this composer. Probably a large proportion of the rest would believe the poll to be merely a practical joke of some kind. These same musicians would probably be astounded to find that Beethoven II was the possessor of undoubted talent, and had composed at least one work worthy of the title "masterpiece," and many others, like this symphony, of great interest. We hope that this recording will help to establish this symphony as a standard work of the concert repertoire.

Perhaps our musicians would ask why a composer of such talent has remained almost completely unknown. We can only surmise that his extremely unfortunate name has quite a lot to do with it. Whether he was named out of an impulse of sadism, or as a genuine tribute to a great composer, we do not know. We know only that it was yet another burden that was added to the many that Beethoven bore throughout his life.

Ludwig van Beethoven II was born in Mannheim in
1828. His father, Hans, was a piano tuner, and young
Ludwig was born into a very musical family. At the age of
three Ludwig began receiving piano lessons from his
father, but the man's dreams of a prodigy remained unsatis-
fied as Ludwig showed little musical talent. As Ludwig
grew up he began to take an interest in law. He begged
his father to be allowed to study at law school, but the man
was adamant, and forced Ludwig to take up the violin.
Beethoven, in his *Scenes from an Unhappy Childhood,* has
touchingly described how he used to get up in the night
and retreat to the little attic, there to read books on law
until the early hours.

Eventually realizing that his entreaties were hopeless,
Ludwig resigned himself to a musical career. His violin
playing improved and his latent musical genius began to
manifest itself; he soon won a grant to study in Vienna.

It was at this point that he was viciously struck by one of
the cruel blows of fate that were to dog him all his life. In
the excitement of leaving for Vienna, Beethoven trapped
two of his fingers in the carriage door. The bones were
broken, and the wound soon became infected. Within a
week he had lost two fingers of his left hand. The remaining
fingers were hopelessly deformed. However, it was this
accident, which seemed so terrible at the time (in his diary
Ludwig writes: "I destroyed my life in a carriage door")
that was responsible for Beethoven turning toward
composition.

His earliest works are uniformly uninteresting, although
one can hear the young Beethoven trying to express his
anger at the injustice of his life, and it is not until the
Fourth Piano Sonata (with its unusual *allegro con dolore*
first movement) and the First Symphony, *The Pathetique,*
that he showed any talent for composition. His next work,
the Violin Sonata, was the first to achieve contemporary
recognition, which it did by virtue of its fascinating slow
movement, the *Marcia Funebre.*

One can see from his writing that at this time Beethoven was going through a very difficult and unhappy time as far as his amatory life was concerned. At the age of twenty-five, after his second broken engagement, he wrote the Konzertstück for Piano and Orchestra, in which much of his youthful suffering was expressed. Although this work is obviously very good, especially the *mesto* middle section, the piece has never been performed in full. Beethoven was never an expert orchestrator: what other composers knew instinctively, he had to study hard to accomplish. In this piece the violin parts in several places would be possible to play only if the violinists were to have the same deformity of the left hand as that suffered by Beethoven. Also, Ludwig suffered from not having learned the piano as a child. There is a great deal of *bravura* in the piano part, but it is clear that Beethoven did not fully understand the limitations of piano playing, and the piece is completely impossible for a single pianist to play. Attempts have been made to play this part utilizing three or even four pianists, but for various technical reasons these have not been a success. Louis Spohr made a little-known arrangement of the work for a chamber orchestra composed of flute, two clarinets, bassoon, wind machine, and strings, but little of the music's splendor comes through.

But, despite his drawbacks as far as orchestration are concerned, it is clear to us today that Beethoven had many progressive ideas about music. One can see from his book *Angst and Music* (now out of print) that he even toyed briefly with the idea of atonality:

Last year I was conversing with my good friend Schoenfeld, when he communicated to me some remarkable ideas concerning the very nature of our art. He felt that for some time now the fundamental part of music, that is its diatonic tonality, had been strained to the point at which it no longer functioned correctly. He mentioned some of the modern composers like Herr Brahms. Although it is clear to me that Brahms is only a fashionable

composer of minor interest, there are other artists of extreme
importance, like Nagel and Fleinstock, to whom this applies with
equal correctness. He explained that the musicians of the future
would develop ideas of tonality that would have no relationship
with our methods of related keys. This music, he felt, would probably be called "non-tonal." I had to concede that he showed
remarkable perspicacity, and felt for a moment that perhaps
it would be in my own interest to begin some works of this
nature, thus being credited with this remarkable discovery, but
owing to a greatly painful hornet sting which I sustained
during the course of the interesting conversation, was unable
to leave my bed for a full week. Schoenfeld again visited me
and told me that he had been diligently applying himself to the
problems involved in the production of "non-tonal" music,
and began to express ideas about a series of all the twelve degrees
of the gamut, which, if I understand his ramblings correctly,
he thought could be arranged in various forms, inverted, back-
to-front, etc., and combined to form both melody and harmony.
It is my own opinion that Schoenfeld was in a feverish state
and had been over-diligent in his studies, and would be well
advised to take a rest in bed. This I told him, and added as a
little joke that perhaps he should have been the recipient of
the hornet's wrath rather than I. He seemed greatly offended at
my words, and since then has not communicated with me.

It was now, in 1853, that Beethoven's parents both
succumbed to a local plague of typhoid fever. Although the
death of his parents was a terrible shock to Beethoven, a
shock that plunged him into despair, at least he had no
financial worries at this time, owing to the fact that his
father, having some years ago invented the iron piano
frame, had amassed a sizable fortune, which he left to his
son.

In expectation of his forthcoming fortune, Beethoven
arranged for a performance of the Second Symphony
(one of his poorest works) which involved eight hundred
and forty performers. The concert was a disaster. Although
the audience was very small, such a riot ensued that mem-

bers of the orchestra were severely injured, the box office
forced open by the angry crowd, and all the evening's
takings stolen. Beethoven was sued for damages by ten
members of the orchestra, and found himself in the position
of owing the total amount for the hire of the hall and the
fees of the artists.

It was a few days after this terrible experience that
Beethoven was informed that owing to a technicality his
father's will had been declared invalid and the money
reverted to the state. Now Ludwig had no way of recouping
his loss, and apparently spent some years in a debtor's
prison.

On coming out of prison, Beethoven found that his
fortunes appeared to take a change for the better. He
received the patronage of Anton Goldschmidt, a wealthy
supporter of the arts and sciences, and also met and fell in
love with Pauline von Birnitz, a lady of high social standing.
Of this meeting Beethoven wrote in his diary: "This
evening I saw an angel, fell, and know that I shall remain
at her feet for the rest of my days." But when Beethoven
began to court the lady's favors, he was somewhat perplexed
to find that her attitude to him was both patronizing and
distant. However, he resolved, with courage, never to cease
his pursuit of her, no matter what the cost to himself. The
touching document he wrote at the time is printed as an
appendix to *Angst and Music*: "Though the terrain be
hard, the privation terrible, yet I have no choice but to go
where she goes, to see what she sees, to breathe the very air
that is perfumed by her presence."

During this period of resolve (not untinged with
optimism), he composed the Fourth and Fifth Symphonies
and also the Serenade for Violin and Orchestra, which was
subtitled: *For Pauline On Her Birthday*. When this last
work was almost finished, he suffered a severe chill which

confined him to his bed, and caused him to be unable to complete the work until several months after the lady's birthday. Her displeasure at his tardiness was increased by her disapproval of the progressive harmony employed in the work, and she promptly broke off her relationship with him. At almost the same time he lost the patronage of Goldschmidt, owing to the fact that Beethoven persuaded him to invest a great deal of money into the wet-plate shadowscopy process, which at that time was seen as a possible alternative to the new science of photography, thus causing his patron to lose a great deal of money.

Beethoven was made prostrate by these two blows. His condition was made even worse when he discovered that his newfound social standing was being destroyed by Fraulein von Birnitz, who was apparently the source of several rumors concerning Ludwig's lack of virility and unusual sexual proclivities, which were at that time circulating through the higher strata of German society.

This was the time of the first of Beethoven's suicide attempts. The composer writes (in *Diary of a Sad Man*):

> One morning I awoke from a particularly troubled sleep, and I knew within myself that this would be my last day in this world. I had a long piece of hemp rope, which I had kept within my view for the whole of the last week, for perhaps I knew that in my extremity I would come at length to this, the only resolution of my grief. I affixed the rope at one end, to a large old beam that ran the length of the ceiling at the top of the house. The other end I fastened into a deadly loop. I stood on a chair, placed the loop about my throat, and offered a brief prayer to my Creator. I looked for a little while at the room which I was so glad to quit, and then stepped without fear from off the chair.
>
> I fell, and was conscious of a strangling blow at my neck, then a frightful pain in my leg as I hit the floor. I felt something strike my back with a fearful blow, and then found myself in the midst of a torrent of falling masonry. For a moment I fancied that I had died and had been taken to the very bowels of Hell itself . . .

Beethoven was not in hell, however, but still in his own home. The beam over which Beethoven had slung his rope was infested with dry rot, and had been unable to withstand the extra strain imposed on it. The beam had split, and in falling, had brought with it half the ceiling. The whole house collapsed to the ground, and it was not until six hours had passed that the rescuers were able to free Beethoven from the wreckage. His life was in the balance for some time, but finally he emerged homeless into the world again, but now lacking his right eye and his left arm.

It was at this time that he began the *Tragic* Symphony, the culmination of twenty years of composition. As his mind had been dwelling recently on the subject of death, he had the idea of giving the symphony a choral movement, the text of which would deal with the experiences of a soul after death, and its judgment before God. Not unnaturally he turned to the work of Heinrich Totenfreund, the dramatist and poet. Beethoven had always greatly admired Totenfreund's work, and believed him to be the most important artist of Germany at that time. In fact it was the work of Totenfreund that first gave Beethoven his interest in literature, an interest that developed into a profound knowledge and understanding.

Beethoven wrote to the dramatist suggesting the idea and, surprisingly, received a very warm and enthusiastic reply, urging him to come to Totenfreund's home in the country to spend a few days there. Beethoven was delighted, and quickly set off for Totenfreund's home. In his diary he briefly scribbled: "To see Totenfreund—this almost compensates me for my suffering!"

Beethoven's joy was to be only short-lived. On arriving at the home of the dramatist, Beethoven was met by grim-faced servants who informed him that Totenfreund had died suddenly that very morning.

Perhaps something of the desolation Beethoven felt at that moment is expressed in the *pianissimo* introduction to the symphony (Ex. 1).

EXAMPLE 1

Beethoven's coach had already left, and another one had
to be summoned from a nearby town. As the hours passed in
waiting for the coach, it is reported that Beethoven's
agitation grew ever more strong. Finally the coach arrived,
and Beethoven climbed in with a strange, jerky-limbed gait,
and they set off along the mountain road. On the way back
to Mannheim, at the highest point of the journey, Ludwig
stopped the coach, walked to the cliff edge, and without a
word cast himself over.

Not yet was he to be allowed the easement of death,
however. Fifty feet down his coat was caught in a bush, and
Beethoven was left hanging over the abyss. It was several
hours before a rescue team arrived from Mannheim, and the
attempt to save Beethoven took a great deal of time. He was
finally brought to the top fifteen hours after he had fallen,
suffering severely from exposure.

In the hospital, he began work on the symphony in
earnest. In music he could release the feelings that boiled
within him—suffering at which we can only guess. In his
hospital bed he planned the symphony—a strangely
constructed work of two movements—and chose his text
from the published works of Totenfreund. It was only a few
weeks before he had completed the draft of the short first
movement, which leads without a break into the large-scale
choral finale.

The opening of the symphony takes place in an atmosphere of desolation and gloom. The double basses intone

their solemn motif, and the violins enter with a hushed tremolando. There is a brief oboe solo which adds to the feeling of timelessness, the falling sixths like stones dropping into the stillness of a stagnant pool.

A cymbal clash heralds the beginning of the first subject proper, but first there is a stirring and oddly familiar horn call in an unrelated key, that reminds one of a general marshaling his forces (Ex. 2). Then begins the controversial first subject.

EXAMPLE 2

There is no doubt that Beethoven's unfortunate name had a great effect on him. One can only imagine the effect that this name, the name of one of the greatest of all masters, would have on the mind of a sensitive composer. Some critics have suggested that Beethoven was influenced by his namesake to an unhealthy degree, and have quoted this symphony, and particularly its first subject, as their evidence. This writer maintains that one has only to listen to the delightful close of this section (Ex. 3) after it has modulated into the E flat major of the forthcoming second subject, to hear the impressive originality of this composer's mind.

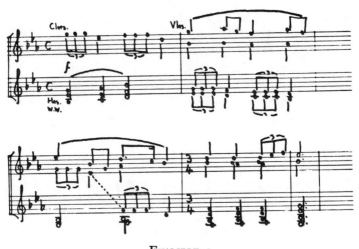

EXAMPLE 3

The second subject is a great contrast. Perhaps the light-hearted nature of the long string tune is due to the fact that at this time Pauline von Birnitz was visiting him at the hospital. Certainly this section is the most cheerful thing that Beethoven wrote, and, at the same time, it demonstrates a remarkably developed melodic gift. There is a fairly short development section, at the end of which the brass blazes forth in a triumphant march. Gradually the rest of the orchestra joins this march, and at its climax the organ enters with a repetition of the double bass motif at the opening of the work.

Then there is silence. The woodwind plays a brief, but hauntingly beautiful chorale (Ex. 4), the bridge from one movement to the next (and perhaps, symbolically, the bridge from one world to the next).

EXAMPLE 4

It is at this point, at the emotional climax of the work,
that Beethoven's music goes beyond the bounds of purely
orchestral sound, and he finds it necessary to introduce
the human voice. The symphony moves into a new sphere
of experience. The vocal entry is surely one of the most
transcendental moments of all music. It is unfortunate
that there exists a certain disagreement about which soloist
should actually sing this part. Beethoven always showed a
distressing carelessness in the preparation of his scores, and
his absentmindedness has here caused a great deal of
confusion. The part of the Soul is marked in the score to be
sung by the contralto soloist. But the part rises at times to
b'', and is clearly beyond normal contralto *tessitura,* as
those performances in which the score has been faithfully
followed, painfully testify. Usually a soprano is given this
difficult part to sing. However, there is a school of thought
which maintains that the part should actually be sung
by a bass, *b''* then becoming *d* (actual pitch). There is
some evidence that makes this claim less preposterous.
Beethoven, at the time he wrote this symphony, had help
from Pauline von Birnitz in preparing the orchestral staves.
It is then easy to see how possible it could be for a double
mistake to have occurred—for Fraulein von Birnitz to
have written "contralto" instead of "bass" and to have
written in the "correct" treble clef; it is also easy to see

how Beethoven, in the white heat of his inspiration, could have missed this error.

Having a bass sing this part, and consequently transposing the intervals by major and minor sixths, certainly changes the character of the music. It removes the grinding dissonance of this solo part, which shocks the mind like a bolt of electricity, and expresses the total alienation of the disembodied soul, and reduces the effect to the banal. On this recording the part is taken by a soprano. It is this writer's opinion that this is the only version that can be taken seriously.

Beethoven followed faithfully the mood of Totenfreund's text (taken from *Canticles and Dramatic Fragments* [now out of print]). Certainly the Sixth Symphony has its faults. Some people maintain that the work's weaknesses outweigh its moments of inspiration: that is for the listener to decide for himself.

Beethoven was to make one more attempt to end his own life. On leaving the hospital he swiftly arranged a performance of this symphony, the work he believed to be his masterpiece. At great expense he traveled to Vienna, and spent his remaining money on hiring the *Konzerthaus* for five evenings. Beethoven was sure that now he would find the public acceptance for which he had craved for so long.

The first performance of the *Tragic* Symphony dashed his hopes to the ground. Beethoven writes: "The hall was unheated, the chorus underrehearsed, the orchestra hostile, and my great symphony inaudible."

From contemporary accounts it appears that the performance occasioned a full-scale riot from which Beethoven was lucky to escape with his life. The performances scheduled from the remaining four nights were canceled.

Standing in the rain outside the empty *Konzerthaus* the next evening, perhaps hearing in his mind the sounds of the closing bars of his symphony and the rapturous applause for which he longed, Beethoven was met by an old col-

league from Mannheim. It was then that Beethoven learned
of the engagement of Pauline von Birnitz to a young rival
composer.

That evening Beethoven returned to his lodgings, after
walking aimlessly about the streets of Vienna, and drank
a great quantity of an oven-cleansing liquid. He was rushed
to the hospital, and after a long and arduous operation
in which half his stomach was removed, he was pronounced
saved.

From this time on Beethoven's life is not at all well
chronicled. Beethoven himself stopped writing his journal,
and there is a singular lack of contemporary writing about
him. We know only that something happened to make
Beethoven change his whole attitude to life. Whether he
had reached the extremity of suffering, which then
metamorphosed into joy, we do not know, but certainly
something caused him to change his outlook. Whether this
experience was an internal or external one we cannot say.
Beethoven himself merely writes, in his last journal
entry: "One must *live!*"

He abruptly began work on the Mass in D, the work
that was destined to be his greatest. Hector Berlioz was
present at the first performance, and wrote in his
Memoires:

Ludwig van Beethoven II has never been taken seriously
as a composer, and deservedly, for there is no doubt that his
work has had grievous faults, not the least of which has been
its singular lack of inspiration. I now say, having heard last
night his Mass in D, that his muse has at last responded, nay,
has veritably heaped upon his head the riches of a lifetime.
With what fluttering intoxication I listened to Beethoven's
music last night! I tore out my hair in a delirium of delight, I
wept, I could not restrain the groans that Beethoven drew
from me! Beethoven says to us, "You must live life to the full,
you must take the suffering and build it into a foundation

for joy, for joy is eternal, and can never die." Here is life herself speaking to us with her full and glorious voice. I say that Beethoven's Mass is one of the greatest of all musical works, and had I written but one bar of this work, then I would have accounted my life worthwhile.

In view of this, it is nothing less than a tragedy that this one performance of the Mass seems to be the only one ever to have taken place. The manuscript appears to have been lost, and has since never been discovered.

Immediately after completing the Mass, Beethoven sustained a small wound to the right thigh, when he fell in the street outside his house. Blood poisoning soon developed, and within three weeks he had died. An ornate tomb was constructed at Mannheim, but it was unfortunately destroyed during the war.

The Text

SOUL: I slept awhile, and now I am awake,
    I see that all that went before was but a dream.
    All is still, and now I understand
    This stillness is the nat'ral state of things,
    And that the flurry of my earthbound life
    Was but the struggle of a soul in flight,
    In fear of drinking at the fountainhead.

    Into my being is poured a magic wine
    Of stillness; now I know
    There's no escape from this, my judgement way.
    The wine has made me like a ship
    At rest from tossing on a busy sea.
    Now I can lift my anchor up and fly
    On snowy wings into the glory of the day.

CHORUS OF MOURNERS: Lord, have mercy on him,
                     Christ, have mercy on him.

SOUL: And down below my friends I see
    Clustered about my bed,
    Knowing not that I, a bird, do fly
    The airy vaults of time,
    My sails outspread, my dipping prow,
    The wine of peace from stern to bow.

    But what is this? I feel that I
    Am urged still further in the sky.
    Did not this solitude so lack
    Another being apart from me,
    And had I now corporeal form,
    I'd say a hand pressed in my back.

ANGEL OF THE LOWER REGIONS: Be thou not feared, O
       little soul,
    'Tis only I, thy humble guide
    Into the regions of the bless'd
    Where thou shalt stand before the throne
    And see thy Father, there to take thy place
    On the heavenly scale, and to be judged and weighed.

SOUL: O blessed one, my gratitude will surely
    Kiss thy face with flutt'ring wings!
    But there is something I would say
    Had I the courage now to speak.

ANGEL: Speak now, my son, for there is nothing here
    To cause you to forbear.

SOUL: Then I will speak; O glorious one,
    I would not try to influence my fate,
    For I would see the Holy One.

But in my earthly life I stood
On many scales, and I do know my weight.

ANGEL: O innocent! O cow'ring soul!
These scales are nothing like the ones you know,
But measure here the worthiness,
The virtue and the grace of he who's weighed.
The denizens of heav'n oft speak rhetorically,
These scales are just meant metaphorically.

SOUL: Now all is clear, as if the world
Were bathed in incandescent light!
My understanding shines forth like a flare,
Lighting up this everlasting night!
Were I so bold, and not so wise,
I'd say that scales had fallen from my eyes.

CHOIR OF PENITENTS: Be gracious in thy mercy, Lord,
This soul that upward flies toward thy face
Is black with sin, but can be purified
By thy stern judgement, thus transposing it
Into the purest white of holy grace!

Praise thee, O Lord, in thy power and glory
Praise thee, O Lord, in thy fullness of eternity
Praise thee, O Lord, in the majesty of thy coming
Praise thee, O Lord, thou highest of the high!

SOUL: And now my angel has departed,
Leaving me alone to swim
In the seas of space and time
When I was getting used to him.

But now a shudd'ring anguish fills me through,
Although I travel on at faster pace.
I shiver, and my being is full of doubt
That I shall see my Holy Master's face.

ANGEL OF THE UPPER REGIONS: Thou shalt not fear, O
    quaking soul,
  Thy pain is nought but agony
  Of incompleteness: thou shalt see his face,
  For my task is to conduct you to his gracious being.
  But the seeing of him you will find overpowering,
  And thy present pain will multiply itself,
  But our most glorious Church has always taught
  Its worshippers to glory in their anguish,
  And many times has added to their pain
  By taking their last money for our altars
  So that they starve, in preparation for the afterlife.
  And when thy pain comes shalt thou too rejoice
  To see the greatness of the greatest one,
  To see His face; to hear His voice.

SOUL: All hail, O being of the higher slopes!
  Your message brings to me great comfortment.
  But I grow now impatient for my moment to begin.

ANGEL: Your patience is no longer needed, soul,
  For we are in the highest air of all,
  Where all is rarified and pure.
  These are the highest bounds of heav'n,
  Where lives the highest one of all.

SOUL: And now I feel myself drawn up
  As if by a power beyond my comprehension.
  A strange convulsion grips my senses,
  A delirium of glory!
  I feel that I have come at last
  Unto the place where I will meet my Lord.
  For this moment was I first created,
  And spent my earthly life so long ago.
  A golden shape before my eyes I see,
  And I know now that I'm approaching Thee!

CHOIR OF ANGELICALS: Praise to the God of ages past,
Praise to the Lord today,
Who made both heav'n and earth and hell,
To help in ev'ry way.

Who sent his only son to us
To labor and to toil,
To spend his life in earthly pain
Old Satan's plans to foil.

Who rules above in glorious might,
With Christ at his right hand,
And spreads his waves of gorgeous pain
All over this fair land.

ANGEL: Brothers! Hist! The soul I see
Descends from the high throne
In pain and wrapp'd in misery,
The judgement now is done.

SOUL: Stand back, O Angels, touch not me,
My pain I cannot tell,
For down I go with utmost speed,
To the very depths of Hell.

ANGEL: Brothers, be not thou downcast,
At this soul's plight thou must not frown,
For though this damned soul plunges fast,
At least we cannot be cast down.

ANGEL OF THE HIGHER REGIONS & CHOIR OF ANGELICALS:
Praise to the God of ages past,
Praise to the Lord today, etc. . . .

The Garden of Delights

HE CLAMBERED DOWN from the bus and stood still for a moment, looking about him as if in bewilderment, while people jostled him from behind. He began to move slowly, conscious of placing one foot before the other, walking along the grass verge. He could see the drive already, half hidden by the hedge, only a short distance from the bus stop. There was a strong smell of foliage coming from the hedges, mingled with the slighter scent of the blooms that stirred gently in the breeze, and perhaps it was this smell that made his memories so acute at this moment. He had nearly reached the drive; it was only a short distance, but it had seemed far when he had been young. Now his feet were leaving the grass, and he was conscious of the feel of gravel beneath his soles. He had a brief moment of near-panic—a strong desire to turn round and leave, and never return to this place. He stood still, afraid to turn the corner, knowing that if he took a few more paces there would be nothing at all between himself and his past. He was suddenly conscious of the utter smallness of his body, sensing the great sky above him and the earth beneath, the galaxy surrounding him, the uni-

verse beyond. He felt as though his body was supporting
a great weight; or rather, as though his mind was
supporting a psychological weight, much less tangible, but
a million times heavier. He staggered forward a pace.
Perhaps the sun was affecting his mind. He put up an
arm to shield his eyes, deliberately walked on, and
abruptly the oppressive feelings disappeared. He smiled to
himself at the intrusion of his own imaginative proclivities
at this particular moment when, after turning this bend
in the drive, it would all be there before his eyes. He
could see the front garden already, and could see that
it was overgrown, a mass of nettles and brambles.
A tree had been choked by ivy.

And now he could see it.

Even in the brilliant light of the afternoon sun the
house presented a forbidding appearance. Although the
front garden was no longer as he remembered it, and
although the windows were broken, and part of the house
obscured by the flank of a bright yellow bulldozer, the
sight of it was still enough to fill him with a sense of
unease, the feeling the house had always given him, and a
kind of horrified nostalgia.

He had not seen the house for nine years. He was
unable to explain to himself why he had come back here,
when by this time next week the house would no longer
exist. He had few happy memories of the lifetime he had
spent here, and these were destroyed by the horror of his
mother's death, and the family's precipitate departure
after the compulsory purchase order.

The wall that had surrounded the front garden now lay
in rubble among the thistles and the overgrown privet
bushes. Although he wanted nothing more than to see the
house reduced to a pile of rubble, yet he had the strange
notion that in demolishing the house, the workmen
would be destroying something of enormous importance
that transcended the physical presence of the building;
something that could never be created again. Perhaps it

was that this house, in which he had spent his first
fourteen years, represented his life, and that the workmen's tools would be destroying not only a building, but
his childhood.

Despite the evidence of destruction, on this Sunday
afternoon there was a feeling of peace over the whole
scene. The decaying building looked as though it would
continue to decay, finally dying a natural death and
turning into an overgrown mound, being absorbed into
the undergrowth, and becoming part of the countryside.
It was strange to be standing here like this and seeing
the house, its brickwork lit by the sun, its walls beginning
to succumb to the ivy, hearing the birds singing in the
trees; it had a feeling of calm that had never been in
evidence while he was living there. Perhaps the tension
had come, primarily, from his parents, who lived in a kind
of truce of coexistence, a truce which concealed a strange
mixture of hostility and compassion.

His earliest memory. His mother, not as she must have
been then, but as he remembered her later—the drawn
face of an old woman. She sits in a chair, her head resting
on the back. He plays with a model car on the carpet
at her feet. The lines of the pattern have become roads; a
matchbox is a garage. She is wearing blue slippers. His
father has come in from his special room—the one he is
not allowed to enter.

"Marcia, where the hell are my papers?" A loud voice.
An angry voice. He feels frightened.

"Which papers?" His mother's voice is very quiet.

"There was a green folder, with a large plan and some
papers on top of it. What the hell have you done with it?"

"Oh those; I put those in your cupboard on the
right."

"Why do you always feel it necessary to move my
things?"

"I've got to clean up, haven't I?"

"Clean up? Clean up? I wouldn't mind so much if you
did clean up! You haven't touched this place for I don't
know how long. It's filthy. Filthy! There's dust an inch
thick in my study. There's a sink full of washing-up.
I don't know what's come over you lately; at one time
you kept this place spick and span, now you don't seem
to care about what kind of conditions we live in."

"I'm sorry, darling, I don't know what's wrong; I've
been so tired lately."

"Tired? I'm tired too. Tired of trying to bring up a
young child in a pig-sty." His father's voice suddenly
becomes more gentle. "Look, why don't you go round
and see the doctor in the morning? He'll be able to give
you a tonic or something."

When his father leaves the room, he suddenly feels
tears running down his face. He is taken up, and is
surrounded by his mother.

"There, there, my darling Robin, don't cry. He doesn't
really mean it."

He buries his face in her softness, and gradually his
unhappiness gives way to warmth and pleasure.

Slates are missing from the roof. There is a slight
smell of decay coming from the building. The lawn, once
a neat oval in front of the house, is now a shapeless
patch of wild grass and brambles. All over the front of
the Georgian building, paint that was once white and is
now a shade of grayish cream, is peeling in great swathes
from the plaster. It is strange that at the period in the life
of a building when time is most critical—the moment at
which demolition has just begun—it should look so
timeless. It was as if this house had always been here,
and would remain forever—an unalterable fact of
existence, like a mountain or an ocean. He walks across
the garden, brambles whipping at his legs, and stands
before the front door.

His mother has gone away, and has been gone for ages.
He feels very unhappy, as if he will never see her again.
His brother, who sleeps in the room next to his, and
who is nearly as grown-up as his father—a fourteen year
old, nothing like a baby of five—has been very sad as
well; he can tell. He is in bed, and Daddy comes up to
see him. He can remember only a little of this conversation.

"She is very ill. She will be coming back here the day
after tomorrow, but she's had a very serious operation,
and she will have to spend a lot of time in bed. Now I
don't want you to worry her in any way. She must have a
great deal of rest, and I'm going to make sure she gets it.
So you'll have to be very, very good."

"Why is Mummy ill? She hasn't done anything."

"People get ill; they don't have to be very bad."

"I think God is wicked to let Mummy be ill."

"Now don't say things like that. If we both pray for her
as hard as we can, she may be quite better soon."

His father had left, and he had been very unhappy.
Instead of saying his usual prayers that night he had said,
"I hate you, God, for making Mummy ill, and I think
you are very wicked. I'll kill you, God!"

The glass in the front door had been smashed, and now
one could see through into the blackness of the hall.
Inside, he could see dirty floorboards, and the broken
plaster of the walls. Over one of the smashed panes there
was a translucent spider web, moving gently in the air.
Now he was so close the house looked much smaller than
he remembered it. This gave him a feeling of security,
a sense that his memories could no longer hurt him. He
wondered again about his motives in coming here. On
hearing that the council were at last going to go ahead
with the main road, after an even longer than typical
delay of nine years, he had felt an imperious summons to

return here, as if it were essential that he have this final meeting with the house. As if, perhaps, he would learn something here, something he had never learned in all the years he had lived here.

He pushed open the front door, and it swayed in at a crazy angle, its top hinge no longer attached. The hat stand was still there, where it always had been; many things that his father had deemed useless had been left behind in their hurried, unnecessary departure. Even the mirror was still there, but it had been smashed, and broken pieces of glass littered the floor. He stepped inside the hall, conscious of the now-strong smell of damp plaster and decay. Bricks lay scattered all over the floor, and someone had written obscenities in bright red paint all over one of the walls. To the right the staircase still swept upward, but now many of the bannisters were missing, and he could see a hole in the tread of one of the steps. A piece of flex dangled down at the site of what once had been an elaborate light fitting and, in the corner, a piece of ceiling had fallen down, and now laths were exposed, like the ribs of the house's skeleton.

But it was only the surface that had shifted. All was basically the same. The stairs still curved round; the door to his left still indicated the lounge; another door further down on the right still concealed a large cupboard that filled the space under the staircase; the door at the end of the hall on the right was still the entrance of his father's study. He wondered why, then, he was not filled with the feeling of nostalgia that he had experienced so strongly when he had first caught sight of the house. Perhaps these small changes were enough to blunt the edge of his recollection. Perhaps the bricks littering the floor had at last broken the forbidding atmosphere of this building. There was one room he hoped had not changed; his mother's bedroom.

He is sitting on the sheet. "So we all waited for him down by the bridge, and then we got him and bashed him up!" She puts her head back and laughs, and then sweeps him against her.

"I know he is a bully, and he was fifteen and you're all only eight, but it's wicked to fight, and you mustn't anyway." She looks down on him. "Your face is too lovely for me to see it all cut and bruised." She touches the sore spot on his face.

"It's only a little bruise, and anyway he ran away."

She laughs again, and with his ear against her breast, he can hear the laughter rumbling in those great mysterious spaces inside her where, even now, he knows, a terrible disease is eating her away.

In that room he had seen her for the last time, with the face of an old hag, pieces of cotton wool stuffed into her nostrils, her flesh white and cold, and her face drawn into an expression that could have been a smile or a grimace of agony. But now, he wanted to see the room for all the memories it had—not just to remember the times when she had looked younger, for he could only remember her as a woman made prematurely old by illness; in those earlier days he was sure that she had been beautiful—not to censor his memories, but to remember all, all the pain and unhappiness, so that he could stand and soak in the totality of what his mother had been.

He turned, and began to walk carefully up the stairs.

With the make-up removed, he could see that she was beautiful. And she was young, much younger than he had throught at first. Her face was oval, and gave a remarkable impression of serenity. She had large eyes, and the colored light was reflected in her gaze as she looked at him intently. Her nose was straight, and it flared at the bottom into wide nostrils, which he could see were moving

with the deep breaths she took. Her lips were full, but
pale. Her face was full of paradoxes. It was a face that
showed a deep sensuality, but at the same time a basic
serenity of soul; it showed, in her high cheekbones and the
set of her features, a great deal of strength, but at the
same time a frightening frailty. She was young, but at
this moment she seemed to be ageless, a monument, a
figure of legend, as if time no longer had any meaning, as
if her beauty could never fade.

A strong gust of wind set the lanterns swaying, and he
watched the play of colored light across the planes of her
face. Everything he saw seemed to have an almost fright-
ening significance, a meaning not usually attached to the
mundane things of the world. Her dark hair, the swinging
string of lanterns, the feel of the wind on his skin, a
garden bench with a support broken in its back, the
branches above them, moving slowly back and forth.

"I feel," he said slowly, breaking the long silence
between them, "that in this garden there is—everything.
As though all the time in the world has been gathered up
here, and that this night will be an eternity for us."

"As though there is nothing," she said, her voice quiet,
and almost drowned by the sighing of the leaves, "noth-
ing at all in the world that can hurt us at this moment.
That nothing exists apart from this moment. That we are
the only breathing people in a world that is somehow
our own world."

There was a gust of laughter from the house. Through
the french windows he could see people moving about
inside the brightly-lit room.

"How old are you?" he asked, not believing that she
had an age.

"My dear sir," she said, with an odd, half-hearted
parody of primness, knowing that it was a question he had
to ask, "that is hardly a polite question for a young lady
to answer. But I'm nineteen."

"I'm twenty-three," he said. "I don't think I've ever
seen anyone as beautiful as you."

"What are you called?"

"Robin."

"Robin. Robin. I love you, Robin."

"And I love you."

There was a tinkle of breaking glass from the house,
and another roar of laughter. Reclining, as they were, on
the grassy slope, their heads were turned toward each other,
and her eyes were still fixed on his.

She spoke again.

"I feel that I ought to laugh at this strange conversation we're having. I've never spoken like this in my life
before. It's as if it's hardly me that's speaking; as if I'm
taking part in a play, and the whole scene is laid out before
me. I ought to laugh, but at the moment I feel as though
I won't be able to laugh again, ever."

As the french windows were opened, a flurry of conversation could be heard. He glanced up, and saw a group of
people standing in silhouette outside the french windows,
all carrying glasses in their hands.

"We can be seen from here," he said.

She looked up.

"He'll kill me if he finds us. Let's go further down."

He stood up and helped her to her feet. He could feel
her warmth through the chiffon of her dress. He put his
arm round her, and they walked down the slope into the
darkest part of the garden. Here the light from the lanterns
reached only faintly, and cast a pale glow on the far wall.

"Here is our place," she said, and she pulled back the
branches of a thick bush, slipping through the space
between the bush and the wall.

He could see ahead of him, the skin of her back, the dim
flesh touched with the pale colors of the lanterns' light,
concealed at her waist, where the lines of her dress—begun
at her shoulders by the straps—met, hiding her body

from his view. He could see, beyond her, a little sheltered patch of grass, almost totally invisible from the lawn. He knew, as he began to follow her into the arbor, that he would never experience anything like this ever again . . .

He stood looking at the door of his mother's room. To the right, fungus was growing in a riot of orange along the skirting board, like the cancerous disease that had grown in his mother, until she could live no longer. He had been fourteen. It had been such a long disease. He remembered how, after she had died, he had been plunged into a world that seemed to have no meaning for him. When the wind blew in his face, it was a sensation of the skin. He was conscious of his eyes seeing, his ears hearing; it was as if the real person had curled up inside him, and was now far removed from the interpretation of these purely physical stimuli. It was a paroxysm of mourning, a mourning that had lasted for years. He was not sure that it was yet over.

Her blond hair was spread on the pillowcase, and the smell of her body was strong as he entered her. She wriggled beneath him, and he was conscious only of distaste, and of the rising muscular tension of his body. His spasms began and in his mind he counted them until his body was relaxed again. She lay quite still. He removed his penis, and carefully wiped it with his handkerchief. He looked at his watch.

"You're not," she said with heavy sarcasm, "exactly a Casanova, are you?"

In the alleyway he was suddenly conscious of the movements behind him. There were many of them. There was still time for flight, but he couldn't be bothered. He turned.

There were four of them, large men, and they advanced

threateningly. They had probably mistaken him for
someone else. He stepped forward and was immediately
plunged into a maelstrom of blows. He hit hard, not
caring that he was being hurt as well. He kicked at
someone's groin and heard a scream of pain. He felt
something splinter under his fist, something else that was
soft. And then there was a sudden release of pressure, and,
abruptly, he was free. Three men were running down
the alleyway. One man was lying on the ground clutching
his crotch, moaning. He spat blood, and found a loose
tooth with his tongue. There was blood dripping down
from his face all over his clothes.

He was really quite badly hurt.

*He spread his jacket out on the grass, and they sat
down. There was now no more noise from the house;
everything was still.*

She spoke. "Do you mind if I have a cigarette?"

"No. Of course not."

*She felt into her bag, brought out a pack of cigarettes
and offered him one.*

*He refused the cigarette, but then reached forward and
caught her arm, bringing the packet into a patch of light.
"Minors? Do they still make those?"*

*"Oh, don't!" He too caught her distress, and he felt it
as if a sudden cold wind had disturbed the warmth of the
evening. She placed the cigarette in a long holder, lit it,
and moved closer to him, so that he could feel her
warmth. "What are we going to do about this, then?"*

"This?"

*"This situation. Are we going to make love here, and
then go back to the party? Am I going to say to him,
'Darling, it's all off, I met a strange man in the garden and
love him. Call off the party, there's no longer an engagement to have a party about?' Are we going to make love
here and then try to forget each other, and marry other*

*people, and know that something forever will be missing
from our lives? Or shall I go back to the party now, and
try to forget that this ever happened?"*

He spoke softly. "You can go back if you want to."

"You know that I can't."

*He sighed, and lay down beside her. She shook her
head, then stubbed out her cigarette on the grass, and lay
back, inside the curve of his arm. The feel of her was
electrifying. The flesh of her shoulders was enough to fill
his body with an imperious erotic hunger. He leaned
over her, and looked down at her face. She was breathing
deeply, and her eyes were liquid.*

She put up a hand and stroked his face.

*"Where have you come from?" she whispered. "You and
your funny clothes. Why did you come? My life has been
so simple up to now—I just don't know how to cope with
this. Oh God, why did we have to meet like this?" She
turned her head sharply away from him, and now he
could see only her short dark hair, her ear, and a pulse
throbbing in her neck. He put out a hand and gently
pulled her head back. Tears were running down her face.
He slowly lowered his face to hers, and found her lips with
his own. He knew, as he felt the softness of her lips and
the tip of her nervous tongue, that this night would be
the high point of his life, and that after this, there would
be nothing.*

He put out his hand to the door handle. He had to
force the door open—over the years it had become warped
—and then, on his right, he could see the bed. His
mother's bed. The bed on which she had died, having
refused point blank to enter a hospital, knowing that this
was to be her deathbed. Now, after nine years, it stood at a
crazy angle, although it was still in the position in which
it had always been. He remembered his father going in
and out of the room, especially during the last year,
carrying trays of food, books for which she had asked,

bedpans covered with a white cloth, or even the small
cardboard box which apparently contained photographs of
them together, during their engagement and wedding that,
toward the end, she had asked for frequently. Despite
their many arguments and rows, during the long and
inexorable course of her illness his father had nursed her,
if not with devotion, then with patience until, the day she
lay dead in this bed, his duties had been completely
discharged. Then a new briskness had come over him.
They had gone, for a short while, to stay with an aunt,
and then had moved to a flat in the suburbs of London.
The three years he had spent in that flat had been almost
intolerable. During the whole time he had felt nothing but
a near-hatred for his father. All the time, he knew, he
was blaming him for the death of his mother, and this
feeling, while illogical, was powerful and grew more so,
until he finally left, and went to live in a small flat in
Kensington. The year after that his brother, then twenty-
six, married, and his father was left to live alone. Now that
the man was lonely and showing his age, he found it
impossible to hate him, and visited him every week. Now,
the only reminders of the days of his mother's life were
this house and this room.

She is lying back in the bed. He looks down at her
face. It is thin, the face of a skeleton. Her skin is wrinkled
and old, like the skin of an old woman, but with a yellow
shade not normally seen in the flesh of living people.
Her hair, gray and tangled, lies all over the pillowcase.
He puts out his hand and strokes her brow.
"Oh Robin, I've been thinking so much about you
during the last few months. I've been worrying about
certain things for years, and—"
"You shouldn't worry, Mum, you know it's bad for
you. If you rest and take it easy, perhaps you'll be on your
feet again one day."
"Oh Robin, Robin, I wish you wouldn't humor me.

Or yourself. I'm never going to be on my feet again. You
know as well as I do that it won't be long before I die. I
can accept it. You'd probably be surprised if you knew
what a little thing death is for me. I've never clung to
life—never felt it was worth clinging to. At least, not since
I was a young girl."

"Oh, don't talk like that, Mum." There are incipient
tears in his eyes, and he feels a sense of panic, as he
does every time she speaks of her own death.

"Oh, I'm sorry love." She reaches out and draws him
close. She lifts up a hand, and gently runs it over his
cheek.

"When I look at you I—Oh Robin, if you only knew
what I sometimes fancy to myself lying here . . . But it's
just the ravings and flutterings of a dying woman's mi—"

She convulses in a spasm of pain, and a loud cry is
forced from her. He feels his own face twisting too, in
imitation of her agony. He quickly goes to the door of the
room and calls, hearing his cry echoing through the house
and echoing through his numb brain, as it has many
times before.

"Dad! Dad! Come quick, she's in pain again!"

*She is lying back on his jacket. He can see her face
below in the shadows, illuminated by a single spot of light
that filters through the leaves. Her face is given a pale
phosphorescence, like the face of a Madonna. He lowers
himself to her. They kiss with urgency, and he thrusts his
body against hers. As his mouth travels the skin of her
face, her ear, her neck, her shoulder, his hand pushing
the shoulder strap down her arm, he feels overwhelmed
by what he is experiencing, as if he is perpetually on the
point of fainting. Her lips are moving over his neck, and
her hands run over his chest and back as if she were
eagerly trying to trace the contours of a piece of sculpture.
His hand finds the shape of her breast beneath the dress.*

*He can feel the nipple clearly, and as it hardens under his
fingers, he realizes that she is not wearing a brassiere.
He unbuttons her dress, lowers the shoulder straps, and
uncovers the upper part of her body, as if he were helping
a bud to blossom. They clutch each other, and now he
can feel her flesh with his hands, his arms, and his lips. She
unbuttons his shirt, kissing his flesh with every button,
lower and lower. He feels her thighs under the dress, and
feels that she is wearing elaborate garters. He rolls her
stockings down her legs, and then runs his hand back up to
her thighs, hearing the catch in her breath. The backs of
his fingers brush between her legs. Her hand is over his
prick, and he is filled with an infinite sweetness. He has
never known sensations like this before; it is as if their
lovemaking has released a mechanism that until now has
been still. Now the levers lift, the wheels spin, and the
machine rolls off across the universe, tilted and crackling.
He pulls the dress over her head, and sees that she is
wearing long, wide, silk knickers. He laughs, his laugh like
the humor of the cosmos, and pushes his head between
her legs, rubbing his face all over the silk. And now, as
he kisses her thighs, and feels the smooth surfaces of her
bottom, drawing down the silk pants, he can feel her
pulling his last remaining garment over his legs. Now they
are both naked, and dimly he can hear the sound of a
bird and muted noises from the house party, but he is
conscious only of her scented nakedness, of her hands
moving on his flesh. He gently parts the lips of her cunt,
and then lowers his mouth to the soft flesh, feeling, at the
same time, her mouth, a sensation of such exquisite
pleasure that it is almost beyond bearing. As his mind
registers that she is in fact a virgin, and an answering
thought expresses the part of his mind that knew this
already, he is too busy to heed it, his frantic tongue
traveling over the salty flesh in its quest and his quest to
know her.*

It is dark in his bedroom. There is very dim moonlight, but it serves only to change the room into a collection of frightening shapes. He can hear the tick of the big grandfather clock in the hall; a little while ago it struck eleven. He can also hear the voices of his parents. All day Mum and Dad have been angry with each other; they hadn't said anything bad, but it was easy to tell. He shivers in the bed. He doesn't like Dad shouting at Mum, especially as she's not been well for so long. Two years, what a long time to be ill! He wonders if she will always be ill, will always have to go to bed and rest in the afternoon, will always look so tired. His parents always seem to be angry with each other lately, and yet last year, when they said the war was over, he thought that everything would be all right from then on, and that they would always be happy, and that Mum and Dad wouldn't be angry with each other any more, and that Mummy would get well again. But here he was, hearing their voices raised in anger as he had so often before. He snuggled down in the bed, and tried not to listen. But the sounds they made were too intrusive, and he couldn't ignore them. He sometimes prayed to God when they shouted at each other, but God didn't make them stop, and he found that he didn't like God as much as he had when he'd been little. His stomach was twisted up again, and he would have to go along to the lavatory. He swung his legs out of the bed, and dropped quietly to the floor. He put on his slippers and made his way across the room, taking care not to bump into the table, and opened the door. The landing was very creepy, lit, as it was, only by the stray light from downstairs, and he went as quickly as he could to the lavatory. Once inside he switched on the light and bolted the door, feeling much safer. It was then, as he was sitting there, that he had an idea. He remembered that as he had come along the landing the voices of his parents had been much clearer. If he were

to go downstairs and sit on the staircase, he would be
invisible from the lounge if the light was on and the door
was open, and he would be able to hear what his parents
were saying.

He wiped his bottom rather ostentatiously, pulled up
his pajamas, and then pulled the chain, making sure he
was outside before the lavatory made that loud sucking
noise. He could still hear his parents' voices, so they
hadn't heard the sound of the lavatory.

He made his way back along the landing, and then, step
by step, began to descend the staircase, trying hard not
to make any creaking noises. Although the door of the
lounge was shut, he could still hear the voices quite
clearly. When he was nearly at the bottom of the stairs he
stopped, and listened. He heard his father's voice first.

"I've tried. I've tried, but what do you think it's like
for me?"

"Can't you show me any kind of consideration at all?"

"I try to make allowances. I even try to retain some
kind of emotional equilibrium over the children, which is
more than you do. By all accounts I should hate Jack and
love Robin, but I've tried not to be influenced by the
past, and I try to think of Jack as my own son. I think
I've succeeded. But you . . . I can't understand it. First
of all it was Jack you were all over—he was the only one
you cared about; Robin was just an unimportant interrup-
tion to you—"

"That's not true!"

"But now, now you've suddenly started turning all
your maternal charms on Robin, and you're well on the
way to turning him into some kind of pouffy mother's
boy!"

"That's not true and you know it! And if you'd just
try to understand how—"

"Understand? Understand? How many men would

understand the fact that at the altar their bride was three
months pregnant by another man?"

"Oh, we've been through all this so many times before!
I *tried* to tell you, you know I did, but you wouldn't
listen to me. And after that it was no use. I didn't care
whether I married you or not; I just felt *sorry* for you."

"Understand. My Christ! And if it had been a proper
affair it might have been a bit easier to understand. But it
was a casual pick-up, wasn't it? A quick fuck in a bush."

"Oh don't torture yourself with it! It was over fifteen
years ago. You know there's never been anyone else since
then. And if I've begged your forgiveness once I've begged
it a thousand times. I know I was wrong. I know it was a
terrible thing to do to a man. But what have I got to do?
What can I do?"

"I'll never forget, as long as I live, one thing that
summed up your whole stinking attitude. I agreed. All
right, we would think of the child as ours, not as a result
of his mother's fucking around. And then you told me
what you were going to call him. You didn't even ask me!
My God, are you surprised that I put my foot down?
You're lucky I let you have your way with Robin;
although why the name was so important to you I don't
know, although I suspect. If my suspicions were correct
I don't know what I'd do—but I don't want to think of
that. What I am objecting—"

"Why? Why are your persecuting me like this?"

"Me persecuting you? Ha! If ever the day will . . ."

Robin didn't understand what his parents were saying
to each other, but he felt vaguely that they were angry at
him and Jack, and he felt tears welling up in his eyes.
Trying to choke back his sobs, so that his parents wouldn't
hear him, he went quietly back upstairs and climbed back
into bed.

He walked slowly out of his mother's room, and went
back down the staircase, avoiding all the missing treads.

Once in the hall he went toward the back of the house,
stepping over piles of bricks, and trying to avoid the holes
in the floor. The kitchen was a shambles, with the door
no longer there, and broken glass all over the floor. The
sink had been pulled away from the wall, and had been
smashed into chunks of porcelain. Now he was beginning
to feel very depressed as all the changes really began to
register with him. At that time his life had been bad—
he had often been very unhappy—but still it had the kind
of qualities that were so lacking in his existence today.
He had come from a life of deep miseries but sudden
joys, and was now in a strange flat land, a hinterland of
the mind, in which the weather was always gray, the
climate bland, and the population unimportant.

He went out of the kitchen entrance, into the back
garden. He was horrified at the changes that had occurred
here. He had always loved the garden, and had spent much
of his time here, and he hated to see it in such a state of
bareness. The front garden had been overgrown and
luxuriant, but here the predominant colors were brown
and yellow. There was a terrace at the back of the
house, and then a paved path led right down, almost the
whole extent of the lawn. The lawn was now covered by
scrubby grass and a few bushes. The path was uneven,
and he walked carefully along it. The flower beds were
almost indistinguishable from what had been the lawn;
they now displayed nothing more than stringy nettles and
yellow grass. The garden now had a depressing aspect once
peculiar only to the house. The only things he really
recognized were the metal lamp standards that flanked
the path, some of which were by now very crooked, the
fountain, past the end of the path, just before the lawn
sloped down to the far wall, now dry and cracked, the
garden bench on the right, and the little cherub statue at
the end of the path. He patted the cherub's behind, as if in
condolence.

By now it was impossible to convince himself that she
had much more time to live. Death was written on her
terrible face, lined with years of agony; death was written
in the movements of her crabbed hands as they plucked
and pulled at the sheets. It was there in the constant
spasmodic pain, relieved only by frequent morphine
injections; in the shouts and groans that she was no longer
able to prevent.

Today she was very agitated. Her mouth quivered like
the mouth of a senile old woman. There were egg-stains
on her nightdress. She gabbled something at him, but
he was hardly able to hear what she said now, and
she dribbled saliva down her chin. He wiped her mouth,
and said, "Just try to lie quietly, Mother."

She writhed on the bed in what looked like a parody of
impatience, and then screamed briefly as she was struck
by another convulsive wave of pain.

"Robin! Robin!" she was calling.

He hoped that she was not going to have a really
bad spell. It was strange how one became so detached from
someone in this condition. It was as if one could divide
one's mind into compartments, so that his mother
would be on one level, and this gibbering, scarcely-human
creature on another. Perhaps this was just defense
against the pain she was suffering. There was no pleasure
at all in the life she had remaining; just a declining
resistance to pain.

"Robin!" she called, only quieter this time. Her breath
had been rasping very badly for the last two days, and
now, it suddenly seemed to be much worse; it was as
though she was having difficulty in breathing at all.
He wondered if he should call his father. He made a move
toward the door, and then was horrified to feel a hand
clutching his arm. He looked back and saw that his
mother was sitting up in bed looking at him with piercing
eyes. He stifled the revulsion he felt at her clutching

hand, and turned back to her. Was she looking at him, or
was she looking rather at something in her own head?
She had not been strong enough to sit up for months.
What had happened?

"Robin," she said in a clear voice. "Robin, my darling,
I love you." And then the hand tightened briefly, painfully, before relaxing and falling away.

She had fallen back on the bed, her eyes still open,
still with a strange, intent expression on her face.

She did not move.

He was in no doubt at all that she was dead.

To add the final indignity to her end, from under the
sheets came the sound of a liquid fart.

She was dead.

She was dead.

He would never see her again.

*Now he was filled with a desire to be in her; a desire
that was pulling his prick toward her thighs, and a desire
was in her that was thrusting her body toward him.
He had wanted to prolong their love-making as much as
possible, but they were no longer able to remain two.
He lay on top of her, looking down at her face. He
moved closer, touched, penetrated a fraction, and she
winced. He remained still for a while, all the time with his
eyes fixed on hers, knowing that his eyes were communi-
cating the same message that he could read in her gaze.
A little more, and she gave a small gasp of pain. He began
to withdraw slightly, but her head turned from side to
side. "No . . . no . . ." she said, and he felt her fingers
digging into the flesh of his buttocks, urging him forward.
He moved, in response to her fingers, and slid inside her,
while she caught her breath and bit her lip. And he was
there. This was where he belonged. It was just like coming home. He had never felt this with another woman,
that here, in the soft wet spaces of her vagina, was the*

*very place for which he had been made, that their bodies
had been designed to fit together perfectly, as if once they
had been one creature; a single unit, and that some time
in the pàst they had been cruelly parted.*

*But now they were together, and they lay there quietly,
looking into each other's eyes, feeling the sensations of
each other's bodies, sensations that they had never
experienced before.*

"I think I am a virgin, too," he said.

He was to see her tomorrow; now, in bed, he was
trying to visualize her face in his mind. But it was impossible. Nothing would come clear in his head; his thoughts
were swirling like gas over a bog. Death was so cursory;
he wished there was something he could do to express
the numb dismay he felt at this moment, and to honor his
mother's name. It was as if the world was due to end,
and had not, and he was still here, but feeling as
unsuited to life as a frog in a desert. Planets should have
cracked, galaxies collapsed, the whole universe slid down a
vortex and disappeared. But here he was, lying in bed,
and the rest of his life was spread out before him like
a long straight road, with featureless countryside on
either side. Soon there was to be the funeral, a ludicrously
inappropriate ritual, and then he would become one of
those people who are obsessed by a small patch of
ground; whose life revolves round the burial-place of the
dead. But perhaps there was something he could do.
Perhaps he could pay her his last respects in his own way,
in his own words, not repeating the chanting doggerel
of some priest.

He climbed out of bed, naked and shivering, and got
into his dressing gown. He quietly opened the door of
his bedroom, and stood listening intently. There was no
sound from his father's room. He moved out on to the
landing, and then made his way carefully to his mother's

room. He listened outside for a while, then opened
the door and went in.

From now on the moment was ceremonial. Everything
had become invested with a symbolic kind of significance.
Every movement in the ritual must be slow; must be
carried out with great delicacy and understanding. His
every gesture must have some kind of ceremonial meaning.

Although he could see the vague shape of her on the
bed, there was no sense of there being another person in
the room. Apart from the sounds of his own body, the
room was totally quiet. He walked slowly across the room
and stood, for a moment, at the foot of her bed. Then he
turned, and felt his way over to her dressing table.
He felt for the handles of the top drawer, then slowly slid
it open.

Inside were the things he knew he would find. A box
of long, thin candles, some jewelery, and an ornate
crucifix. He opened the box of candles, withdrew one of
them, and lit it. The room was filled with a warm
yellow glow. He walked across the room with the candle
held high above his head, and then slowly placed it to
one side of her headboard.

The men had been at her already. Pieces of cotton wool
had been stuffed up her nose and into her mouth. Her
cheeks were now rounded with a fake vitality that she'd
never had in life. Her mouth was drawn into a horrible
grimace. Her eyes were closed.

He walked with a slow tread back to the dressing
table and lit another candle. There were now hardly any
shadows in the room; all was bathed in a warm even
light. He slowly walked across to her bed with the other
candle held high, and then placed it carefully by the
other side of the headboard. In the same way he positioned
two more candles, one on either side of the foot of the
bed. The bed was now lit by a bright illumination,
and there were no shadows at all on her face. She looked

like a bland effigy made from white wax. He knelt
briefly by the side of her bed, and then stood up and went
back to the dressing table. He picked up a cushion from
a nearby chair, and placed it on the smooth top of the
dressing table. From the jewel box he withdrew a
glittering necklace. Holding it at arm's length, for a while
he watched the smooth light of the candles as it was
reflected a hundredfold in the facets of the little stones,
to produce a ribbon of fire. Then he placed the necklace
carefully in the center of the cushion, lifted cushion
and necklace, and deliberately transferred them to a small
table by the side of the bed. Then, bending forward, he
briefly pressed his lips against the little string of jewels.
He picked up the necklace again, turned, and laid it
across the neck of his dead mother, shuddering at the feel
of her stone-cold flesh. He was not able to fix it at the
back, but tucked the loose ends in at the back of her
neck, and arranged the necklace so that it appeared to be
worn normally. He straightened, then turned, and walked
back to the dressing table. From the jewel box he
selected another necklace, and fixed it carefully and
seriously round his own neck. Then he picked up the
crucifix and, holding it in the palms of flat hands, he
returned to his mother's side. He placed it on the
cushion at the side of the bed. The bed had not been
made for someone to be comfortable in, and the sheets
were tucked in tightly; he loosened them, and folded back
the sheets, so that her green nightdress was revealed down
to the waist. He picked up the crucifix, and reverently
placed it between her breasts, then bent again, and
gave it a lingering kiss. Then he rose, and moved slowly
round to the foot of the bed. He knelt, closing his eyes.

Now he felt that in some way he was in communion
with her, and his closeness gave him a sense of comfort
and warmth. The candles had given the room a sense
of intimacy, suggesting by their yellow light that there was

nothing at all outside the room, that nothing else existed.
He mumbled words to her, not prayers, but words of
love, memories and dreams. The moment was hushed
and magical.

But as he spoke he felt a sudden stirring in his groin,
and a wave of his imperious adolescent sexuality. His
words faltered into silence, and he felt for a moment
horrified, as if he had violated a church. But then, as he
looked at the room, the jewels, the corpse, the ceiling,
yellow with the candles' light, he realized that it was
all right, that it fitted, and he allowed it to go on, per-
mitting himself to be washed by these powerful waves,
his hands going nervously to his erect penis. He took
off the dressing gown, and stood naked at the foot of her
bed. His body was quivering, and his hand moved back
and forward in the rhythms of sex, his eyes fierce, and his
lips whispering to her. He leaned forward, as if in torment,
and with one hand supported himself on the footboard
of the bed, which in turn began to shake slightly, the
jewels at her neck sparkling with this movement. And then
his face was twisted with the waves of an ecstasy that
he had never felt before, and he had to bite his lips to
prevent himself from crying out, and as he came, in a
great wash of colors, and as the young semen fell in
drops on to the bed, he kept his eyes, all the time, on her.

The trees did not have many leaves, even though it
the height of summer; it was as though a strange
blight had fallen on the garden, and living things now
avoided this place. He took his hand from the cherub, and
looked back toward the house. He was mesmerized by
it; it was impossible to take his eyes away. It seemed
that the longer he stayed here, the more meaning the
house seemed to have for him. The picture of the
building as it was, half-decaying, and illuminated by the
afternoon sun, was totally compelling. The house was

gaining, every moment, a strange kind of importance, as if
here was the vortex of a field of forces, and the bricks
were sucking into themselves a vast amount of a totally
intangible material. He had a sudden feeling of being very
close to his past. The house in his memory seemed as
close as the house he was now watching. There was a
flash of darkness in front of his eyes. He was beginning to
get imaginative again. He deliberately cleared his
mind of thoughts.

He could see the terrace, the french windows, the
kitchen, the upper story with the great bay windows
and, in the roof, the smaller windows of the attic. The roof
was very red. The pattern of the tiles reminded him of
the patterns of electronic circuitry, and he could imagine
the roof alive, crawling with strange forces. A flash of
darkness in front of his eyes. He saw that in a way
the house could never really be destroyed, for it was a
little part of the universe, as wide as that, as high as that,
as deep as that, as old as that, and in that section of time it
would exist always. A flash of darkness. He looked at
the roof, and in its patterns he suddenly found a truth
that he had never seen before. He knew that he had
learned something from that red tile, from the whole
house, that would have been unimaginable before.
Darkness. Light again. He sensed that the house was not
the object that he now saw, but a form, a perfect form,
that stretched through the cold winds of time. Darkness—
lights within the darkness. Light. And suddenly he
could see that the darkness he was intermittently seeing,
was just another aspect of this summer light. Darkness
—lights. Daylight. That the sky, when it became dark,
was just another aspect of itself that he had been unable
to see before now. If one holds a photographic negative
over a dark surface in such a way that the light is
striking it at an acute angle, sometimes the image can
be seen as a positive one, and yet, at the same time can be

understood as a negative. Darkness—colored lights—
house—stars. Daylight. The periods of darkness were
becoming more frequent and longer, but he knew that it
was just a matter of his own perceptions, and that
the light sky he kept seeing was, in a sense, just an aspect
of this night, just a subtle shifting of perspective. Light.
The night again. He tried not to allow too many
thoughts to enter his mind, and just to experience these
perceptions. He sensed that too much thought could be
dangerous. Light. The night again. But the flashes of
light were becoming less frequent, and shorter, the
night was drawing in again. He could see the stars, and
he looked at these, waiting for this strange time to pass. A
flash of light. The stars were cut off where the roof
of the house was silhouetted against the sky. A flash of
light in front of his eyes. He could hear a cricket singing
from somewhere in the distance, but as he listened for it,
the sound ceased. Now he could hear only the trickling
of the little fountain. With the light shining from the
french windows, and the people moving about inside, with
radiance cast on the terrace, the house looked quite
beautiful. The scent of blossom was heavy on this July
night, and he drew in a deep breath and looked round, at
the trees, at the lanterns, strung on wires running between
the lamp standards, and at the house. He began to
walk slowly about the garden.

*And as he watched her face beneath him, he began,
slowly, to move. And he felt the world moving with
him, the garden, the blossom, the trees, all taking part in
this vast act of love. She moaned, beneath him, and he
felt his movements to be part of the universe, part of
the gigantic mechanism, the enormous clock, its wheels
as big as a galaxy. And as he moved in her time passed
without either of them being aware of it, but both
sensing the movement of the stars, planets, continents,*

people, atoms, in the movements their bodies were making.
He felt as though he were taking part in a ritual dance,
and that each movement that they made was
recorded somewhere in an enormous tome, in pages of
minute symbols. He was now moving faster, and the sense
of plunging into her body caused him to shake and moan,
as also she was convulsed and crying out, and their
hips, twisting and plunging, were moving of their own
volition, their vibrations making a sound, a song, the song
of the stars.

And then he heard a door opening at the back of the
house, and saw a young woman standing outside the
kitchen entrance. She was wearing a long evening dress,
and was carrying a glass. She stepped out on to the terrace
and looked up at the sky. There was something about
her that was strangely familiar; something about the
set of her body, her attitude, and even from this distance
he found her compellingly attractive.

And then she caught sight of him, and began to walk
down the garden path toward him. As she got nearer
and nearer, as he saw her body moving under the green
dress, as her face became clearer, he began to breathe more
deeply, wanting to take her in his arms, feeling a desire
he had never felt for any other.

She stood in front of him, looking up at him. Her dress,
he could now see, was a very pale green, with a "V" neck
and shoulder straps. She was wearing a simple necklace.
Her hair was short, cropped, with a curl curving forward under each ear.

When she spoke her voice was slow, serious, and
wondering.

"Who are you?"

"I . . . I . . . nobody . . . I don't know." Just who was
he? He spoke again. "Who are *you*?"

"I . . . I can't tell you. I feel that I shouldn't tell you. Please don't ask me to."

Her face was heavily made up, but he could see her large dark eyes, and the shape of her features, and knew that she was very lovely. The colored lanterns moved above their heads, and the changing colors emphasized her attractiveness.

The garden was absolutely still.

"What a strange meeting!" he said.

She smiled.

"You feel what I feel, don't you?"

He nodded.

"I don't know how I know; I just do."

"We seem to know everything about each other," he said. "It's as though we are closer to each other than any two people have ever been before."

"I think we are going to make love."

"Yes."

"I am a virgin, you know. I've never been with a man before."

"This is so strange."

"Oh God, what will happen? I'm going to be married soon. That is what this party is all about. I suddenly don't know whether I love him or not."

"I would like to see you without make-up. Can we take it off?"

She nodded, and moved toward the little fountain. He watched her as she bent over and washed her face, and as he looked at her slim form it seemed to him that her body was at once familiar and strange. He handed her his handkerchief, and she dried her skin. He walked further along the garden, to the slope where the lawn inclined down to meet the far wall, and after a few moments she joined him, lying down beside him, smiling.

With the make-up removed, he could see that she was beautiful. And she was young, much younger than he had

thought at first. Her face was oval, and gave a remarkable impression of serenity. She had large eyes, and the
colored light was reflected in her gaze as she looked
at him intently. Her nose was straight, and it flared at the
bottom into wide nostrils, which he could see were
moving with the deep breaths she took. Her lips were full,
but pale. Her face was full of paradoxes. It was a face
that showed a deep sensuality, but at the same time a basic
serenity of soul; it showed, in her high cheekbones and
the set of her features, a great deal of strength, but at the
same time a frightening frailty. She was young, but
at this moment she seemed to be ageless, a monument,
a figure of legend, as if time no longer had any meaning,
as if her beauty could never fade.

A strong gust of wind set the lanterns swaying, and he
watched the play of colored light across the planes of her
face. Everything he saw seemed to have an almost
frightening significance, a meaning not usually attached
to the mundane things of the world. Her dark hair, the
swinging string of lanterns, the feel of the wind on his
skin, a garden bench with a support broken in its back, the
branches above them, moving slowly back and forth.

"I feel," he said slowly, breaking the long silence
between them, "that in this garden there is—everything.
As though all the time in the world has been gathered up
here, and that this night will be an eternity for us."

"As though there is nothing," she said, her voice
quiet, and almost drowned by the sighing of the leaves,
nothing at all in the world that can hurt us at this
moment. That nothing exists apart from this moment.
That we are the only breathing people in a world that
is somehow our own world."

There was a gust of laughter from the house. Through
the french windows he could see people moving about
inside the brightly-lit room.

"How old are you?" he asked, not believing that she
had an age.

"My dear sir," she said, with an odd, half-hearted parody of primness, knowing that it was a question he had to ask, "that is hardly a polite question for a young lady to answer. But I'm nineteen."

"I'm twenty-three," he said. "I don't think I've ever seen anyone as beautiful as you."

"What are you called?"

"Robin."

"Robin. Robin. I love you, Robin."

"And I love you."

There was a tinkle of breaking glass from the house, and another roar of laughter. Reclining, as they were, on the grassy slope, their heads were turned toward each other, and her eyes were still fixed on his.

She spoke again.

"I feel that I ought to laugh at this strange conversation we're having. I've never spoken like this in my life before. It's as if it's hardly me that's speaking; as if I'm taking part in a play, and the whole scene is laid out before me. I ought to laugh, but at the moment I feel as though I won't be able to laugh again ever."

As the french windows were opened, a flurry of conversation could be heard. He glanced up, and saw a group of people standing in silhouette outside the french windows, all carrying glasses in their hands.

"We can be seen from here," he said.

She looked up.

"He'll kill me if he finds us. Let's go further down."

He stood up and helped her to her feet. He could feel her warmth through the chiffon of her dress. He put his arm round her, and they walked down the slope into the darkest part of the garden. Here the light from the lanterns reached only faintly, and cast a pale glow on the far wall.

"Here is our place," she said, and she pulled back the branches of a thick bush, slipping through the space between the bush and the wall. He could see, ahead of

him, the skin of her back, the dim flesh touched with the
pale colors of the lanterns' light, concealed at her waist,
where the lines of her dress—begun at her shoulders by the
straps—met, hiding her body from his view. He could
see, beyond her, a little sheltered patch of grass, almost
totally invisible from the lawn. He knew, as he began
to follow her into the arbor, that he would never experience anything like this ever again. . . .

. . . and soon they were moving together violently, their
loving now the only fact of the universe. There was
nothing except each other, and they moved like a single
creature.

Their violence in love was a kind of tenderness. It was a
total freedom which they had given each other, a total
trust. He could no longer feel the summer night; he
could feel only her body, his body, he could hear only the
sounds they made. Their movement, too, was a kind of
stasis, a still eternity of sensation, as though they were
both suspended in space, and nothing was happening,
nothing was moving.

But the dance was coming to its conclusion. He was
conscious of a growing sweetness, communicated from
her, as her head began to move from side to side, and
he heard the regular moans coming from her throat.

The feelings grew, widened, became a field of white,
an iridescent snowscape, and she began to cry out, and he
was falling into a void, seeing her face expressing her
sweet agony, and then there was nothing but whiteness in
his brain, and he dimly heard his own cries, and a
scream which was torn from her. And then nothing but
the surges, and for a moment, he felt that he was her
and she was him, and throughout the whistling void of
time they would never be parted.

And then they were still.

This moment after was like death, and they were still
sharing this, having come through the storms together.

Her face was totally blank. She looked as though
there was no more life within her.

And as he lay in her, he began to be conscious again
of the passing of time, and as each minute went by, it was
one minute less of the time they had remaining. And
he knew that there were not many minutes left.

As if she sensed this, she opened her eyes, and gazed
deeply at him.

"Oh darling!" she whispered.

And it was nearly over. He knew that he would have
to get up and put on his clothes, for the time was almost
run out. He withdrew from her, feeling a terrible sense of
loss, and knowing, by the movement of her eyes, that
she felt this too. He stood up.

"Perhaps," she said, still lying in an attitude of abandon, "this has ruined my life. It will certainly affect my
whole future. And yet I know that as long as I live, I
will never regret this."

As he dressed, he looked at her.

"I know. If I never live again, at least I lived tonight
in a way I never have before."

And as he put on his jacket, he knew that he had to
walk back to the cherub. He stood looking at her for
the last time, as she lay with her arms and legs outspread,
like a fallen statue. The swinging of the lanterns made
her body seem to be moving gently, an echo of their
lovemaking. The bushes stirred in a soft breeze. There was
a flash of light.

"I've got to go now," he said.

Her eyes opened wide.

"I know," she said.

He began, slowly, to walk backward away from her,
keeping his eyes fixed on hers. He could see that she was
crying.

"Oh God, Robin," she called, "I hope I'm pregnant. I
hope to God I'm pregnant!"

The branches of the bush were now beginning to hide

her body from his view. A flash of light. But he could
still see her face.

"Goodbye," he said.

A last branch swung into place, and cut off the
communion of their eyes. He felt as though a vital organ
had been torn from his body.

As he walked back to the cherub, through the flashing
lights of his mind, he heard her voice for the last time.

"Robin, my darling, I love you!"

The sun seemed intolerably hot. He was half-blinded
by the light, which was reflected by the tears in his
eyes. He walked over the parched earth, conscious of the
wetness running down his face, and sat on the old
garden bench, the one with the support broken in its
back. He took out his handkerchief, and rubbed savagely
at his eyes, but he was unable to suppress the sobs he was
making. The bush, whose branches he had just pushed
through, was now black and small, and the luxuriant
foliage had totally disappeared. Now he could see past it
into the arbor. Now there was nothing but soil covered
by patches of weed.

He dried his eyes and looked up at the house. No
longer charged with significance, it appeared to him as it
had when he had arrived.

There was a bird singing nearby.

His mind was a maze, but he knew that one day he
would have to piece together all the complex implications
of what had happened. Now, he could only mourn, as
he had mourned her once before.

Had she known, at the end? As she lay dying, and
watched her second son growing older and gradually taking on the appearance of her brief lover, did she think
it was a matter of coincidence, and nothing else?

He began weeping again, his body shaking on the
bench. Life now, after this day, seemed to be intolerable.

But he would have to live. Soon he would leave, and go back to his home in London. If he ever came this way again he would be driving in a car or a coach, along the road over the place where the house had been. And perhaps he would not know its exact location, and would not be able to sense just when the wheels of the vehicle would be running above the site of this house and this garden. And perhaps he would not care; perhaps the hold that the house, his past, his family, and his lover had over him would, from now on, be broken forever.

But even as he thought this, he knew that it was the opposite of the truth.